SEASON FOR SIN

SEASON FOR SIN

LOUIS LORRAINE

CUTTING EDGE

ISBN-13: 978-1-954840-26-3

Published by
Cutting Edge Books
PO Box 8212
Calabasas, CA 91372
www.cuttingedgebooks.com

CHAPTER ONE

THE May moon hung white and full in a star-studded sky. A spring wind stirred the curtains, wafting scents of roses, pine, honeysuckle.

Gerald Franklin stirred restlessly in his wide, lonely bed. He had heard Alice go to her room an hour ago, had heard her take a shower. For a while, she had listened to radio music.

He could not control his desire for her. Before cold reason or pride could stop him, he was out of the bed and at the door connecting their bedrooms.

He hesitated on the threshold.

In the dark, Alice lay motionless, her face in the shadow. The outline of her form was clear under the sheet. His blood stirred. She was his wife. His to embrace when he chose—that was the contract.

He sat on the edge of her bed. "Alice? Are you asleep?"

She turned her head, pushed the dark curly hair away from her face. Her voice was emotionless. "Not yet. What do you want?"

She was not encouraging, but neither was she sending him away. He drew back the sheet boldly, slipped in beside her.

"What do you think I want?" He reached for her with more assurance than he felt.

Her slim body was limp, as usual. He put his hand on one of the soft breasts. She did not move or respond.

He leaned over her, feeling a desperate compound of loneliness and lust. He pressed his mouth to her warm cheek, caressed her throat. She stiffened. He shoved aside the straps of the thin nightdress and bared her breasts.

Her arms lay at her sides.

What was the matter with Alice? Jean would have been rolling her hips by this time, begging him, crying out for his embrace.

He spoke her name, slid the nightgown above her knees, kissed her frantically. He was hungry for her, starved for response.

"Alice," he whispered. "Alice. Honey. Sweet."

She did not move. Her legs were unbending. Her arms were relaxed, like a rag doll's. He caressed her for a long time with his hands.

Finally her stiffness broke a little.

He possessed her.

She did not seem to know he was there, he realized in horror.

He satisfied himself in some minimal physical fashion. Then, "Alice," he begged. "What's the matter? Do I take too little time?"

"Too much time," she said coldly. "I wish you could get it over with more quickly. I give you what you want. Why do you have to prolong things?"

He bit his lip, joyless beside her in the darkness. She made him feel half a man, incapable of rousing a decent woman. Maybe that was the trouble—maybe he belonged with women like Jean Moore, not with Alice Merton, who was capable of snubbing even a husband if she felt he was socially inferior to her.

He would not give up. He was crazy about Alice. She was the girl he had fallen in love with two years ago, a nymph at the lake where other people were mere swimmers, a slim goddess in a red bathing suit, dark eyes mysterious, unreachable. He had wanted her, won her. But what had he won?

People in the town of Merton—named after Alice's family—thought he had married her for money. But he was coming to hate the financial empire her grandfather and father had built for her.

He leaned over her tenderly again, kissed her breast. She was so lovely—she still was the water nymph he had fallen in love with. It had to be his fault that he had not been able to rouse her.

She shrank away. "Stop it," she said. "I don't want you to touch me now."

He lay back, defeated. "Why did you marry me?" he burst out. "You don't want me to touch you. You never respond. What's wrong?"

"Nothing is wrong. Marriage is about the way I expected it to be. The man lusts. The woman submits. So I submitted. Go to bed."

He thought of her hard-headed father and grandfather. Maybe her father's treatment of her mother was the clue to Alice. There had been talk, Gerry knew. He was growing to feel that Alice resented all men, that some psychological hurt had left her incurably frigid.

In addition to Alice's rebuffs, he seemed also to have incurred the town's disapproval—the community cynically considered Gerald Franklin a successful fortune-hunter. If Alice also considered him a fortune-hunter, he would leave her, he vowed. His pride had been torn enough.

But he had vowed that before. Again and again. And always he had faltered before that last final step of leaving his wife.

Gerry had been away from his home town for several years before returning and marrying Alice. After marriage, he had obtained jobs in town, only to have her arrange for him to be fired. She would act discreetly, but everyone knew what was going on. Gerry had gone to the Merton cotton mill a few months ago, begged a job from the manager. He had been refused.

Now even the mill had closed. Men were packing up their families and leaving town. The town was broke. This was the time to walk out—if he could persuade himself to go.

"Why did you marry me?" he insisted. He leaned on an elbow, touched her longingly once more. "Alice, why?"

"Oh, let me alone," she pushed his hand away. "I was almost asleep."

"I'm sorry. But I have to know. Tell me why you married me."

She laughed angrily. He knew she would say something cruel.

"Because you make a good appearance," she said. "Because you make a good-looking host. And you're cheaper than a butler."

Gerry caught his breath in a gasp of shock. She had gone farther than usual tonight.

His pride in ribbons, he rose and stalked to his room. He lay sleepless, tossing from one side of the bed to the other, for the rest of the night. Once, she used to tell him she loved him. But this had sounded more honest. *You make a good appearance.*

Underlying her coldness, he sensed that in her peculiar way she loved him. She had married him, was living with him, had gone berserk with rage and fear the times he threatened to leave her.

But their love was tearing him apart. He was no longer certain that his own love for Alice was wholesome or even moral— even though they were married.

Toward dawn, Gerry fell into deep sleep. When he awoke, it was after eleven—the day was half gone. It would be a half-day like all his half-days, idle, frustrated, sad. He would kill time, maybe have a swim in the lake, followed by a game of tennis with someone else as idle as himself.

He remembered Alice's cold words last night. Suddenly he had to believe she meant what she said. She had married him because he looked like a good host. She did not, could not, love him.

Before dressing, he dialed Jean Moore's number on his bedroom extension.

Jean's husky voice always tended to sound as though she just had been in bed—ornamentally.

"Jean? This is Gerry," he announced himself.

"Hello, darling. Come on over."

"I'm going to pack," he said. "Why don't you pack too, so we can leave this crummy town?"

"Do I hear you right?" she asked.

"You heard me. You've been begging me to do it for two years." He laughed mirthlessly. "Let's go. We might as well go with a bang. I'll be there in half an hour."

"But, Gerry—"

He hung up. If he kept on talking, he would talk himself out if it, as he had so often done in the past. This time was different. This time was final. He was leaving Alice. Leaving this room that was his, not theirs.

He opened the door of his closet, a magnificent mirrored compartment. Once he had laughed at the skimpy row of suits which huddled there like mock poor relations. His pride had never allowed him to buy new suits with Alice's money.

He pulled down a suitcase that was older than his marriage, battered, splashed with old college stickers. He packed in blind despair, slammed the suitcase shut and struggled with the lock.

A note to Alice? No. He would tell Grace Troy he was leaving. Alice would understand why.

At the foot of the stairs he found Grace arranging flowers in a tall pewter vase. Her hair was the same dark-gray color as the vase, he realized suddenly—not black any more.

"I'm leaving, Grace," he said with mock gaiety.

"On a trip?" the housekeeper asked.

"Nope. For always. Bye. Be a good girl." He patted her cheek with a sudden surge of homesickness. He had known Grace all his life, had known and loved this town. It would be harder to leave Merton for good than to leave his wife.

But there was no longer a function for him here, either in a family relationship or a business one.

"Goodbye, Gerry. Take care." She made no more fuss than that.

He walked out, surprised at himself, feeling detached.

At the curb in front of Jean's, he honked the horn of his 1950 sedan. He had refused to give the car up when he married, in spite of Alice's urging. Now he was glad he had it. It would have been difficult to clear out of his wife's life in one of her own expensive cars. He wanted to convince her that he had not married her for her money.

He waited. Jean failed to emerge from the big uncared-for house. With a sigh of frustration, Gerry got out of the car and walked up the rickety front steps to the porch.

She opened the front door. Her blond hair was still in curlers. She wore an overworked pink negligee. In the bright afternoon sunlight, she looked older than her thirty-two years.

Gerry was twenty-six. He had been seventeen when Joan initiated him into the mysteries of sex. He remembered her at twenty-three—the age Alice was now—her flesh smooth and firm, her eyes bright with the fun of being alive. Alice, unlike poor Jean, would be beautiful all her days, mysterious, unknowable—

But no more of Alice.

"My gosh, Gerry, I'm not ready," Jean complained. "I don't know what to pack."

Within, the shabby house was in its usual state of defiant confusion, intensified by Jean's frantic efforts to pack three old oversized suitcases. She sat on one of the suitcases and asked, "Did I get what you said on the phone? Did you mean go away—leave town—or only a trip?"

"Leave," Gerry told her. He shoved some dainties aside to clear space for himself on the couch, reconciled himself to sitting and watching her for a while. The world bewildered Jean and she had adjusted to it by taking her time, not letting herself be rushed into decisions. "We are leaving the fair town of Merton, shaking its dust from our heels, taking off for nowhere."

"But when are we coming back?" Jean insisted. "I've got to know what to pack. And what am I supposed to do about my house?"

"Honey, the bank can handle the house while you're away. I thought we would just pick up and go. If you won't come with me, I'll go alone." He did not trouble to tell her that, short of a lucky break, her house would be of no value to any purchaser and might as well decay without her instead of while she lived in it.

"No." Decision took possession of her. She launched herself at Gerry, sent him toppling among the silky undergarments. She kissed him fiercely. "Not alone. I'll go with you wherever you say."

He lay on his back, her soft bulk spreading next to his body, his head pillowed among pink and black slips. His hand at the back of her neck, he pulled her down roughly to his kiss.

"That's more like it," he acknowledged. "More love and less back-talk is what the situation calls for."

Their mouths met, explored. Warmth rippled along his spine. He tugged at her negligée.

"Gerry, I ought to be packing," she protested vaguely.

He pulled her soft, willing hips into place. Involuntarily, as she did most things, she caressed him until his senses throbbed with longing and delight. They yearned toward one another on the couch. He felt the coming of total physical union, clasped her and held her still while he found ecstasy and release.

The act was swift, exhausting.

She rose, patted her negligée, fastened the belt.

"You want it when you want it, don't you, Gerry?" She nudged his hips affectionately. He watched her, submitted to her attentions, with lazy satisfaction.

She was a good mistress. They had their squabbles, but she never denied him what he really wanted.

"Now I've got to finish packing," she went on placidly. "I guess I'll lock up the house and walk off and leave it. Nobody will touch my old junk."

He was glad to hear her make the evaluation herself.

He felt better now that his walking out was definite. He had little money in his pockets, but he could get a job somewhere. A job would be heaven on earth. "Hurry up," he told Jean. "I want to be out of here and a hundred miles on the road by evening."

"Okay, Gerry." She moved about with more purpose, humming, packing chaos down to a capsule. Her slippers flapped and her robe kept gaping open to her waist. Her big soft breasts, white and full as cucurbits, were tipped in berry pink. He had often laid his tired head on those living pillows. She was a comforting woman. Maybe Alice had never been the type to make him happy.

He turned on a table radio. A male voice was pronouncing news in important tones.

"Get some music, honey," Jean urged. "It makes me nervous to hear all that stuff."

To tease her, he left the news on. She wagged a finger at him in mock-reproval, all the severity of which she seemed capable. The radio contributed more bad news from around the world. Gerry listened with less than half attention until he heard familiar names.

"Wallace Bentley is calling a town meeting in Merton tonight. At noon, the owner of the well-known Merton restaurant announced that the closing of Merton Mill means disaster to the small town fifty miles north of here, unless something can be done at once."

Jean sighed. "There they go again. They ought to give up. This town is dead and everybody knows it."

"Announcement of the closing has hit Merton hard. Businessman Bentley fears the actual death of the town, already down from a population of ten thousand a generation ago to less than five at the last census."

"It's more like three thousand," Jean said. She snapped off the radio. "The mill closing is only the last straw. I heard ten families moved out this week alone. Left their houses standing for bums to move in. I guess that's what I'm doing, isn't it? Frank and Lila next door are leaving soon, Lila told me."

The season was nearly summer, yet everything was dying—love, marriage, the town where Gerry had wanted to spend his life.

"The town's changed an awful lot since Oscar Merton died," Jean chattered on. "Remember the old days? Gosh, the old man was a hellion, but he did things. Lila and I were just saying this morning, if old Merton was around, he would have done something. Seems like there's nobody with backbone any more."

"Backbone?" Gerry echoed.

"You remember Oscar Merton. He used to walk through town and men tipped their hats to him. There's no one they'd do that for, now. And old Ben Merton—oh, my." Jean laughed. "What an old devil—nobody liked him, but they sure did respect him."

Respect. Was that the answer? Memories were flooding back, not of Ben and Oscar Merton, but of their times. They had been feared and hated men, yet their strength had kept this town going.

Gerry had to admit the truth in Jean's words. If there were still a Merton man to run things, the town would not be dying.

The Mertons had gone, leaving only Alice—and the man Alice had married, who was walking out in defeat.

The Franklins—his own people—Gerry thought wryly, were an older family than the Mertons. The Franklins had been in decline before the Mertons ever got here, after a heady past that included the American Revolution. In childhood, Gerry had known that his blood lines were excellent and his family no longer important or impressive.

"Maybe I could do something," he heard himself say aloud.

"You?" Jean's honest astonishment was more damning than any criticism. "What could you do, Gerry? The town is dying.

You were right the first time. Let's get out and live it up somewhere else."

"That's what I mean to do," he said. "But I can wait long enough to talk to Wallace Bentley."

"What difference does it make to us?" Jean rolled a pink print dress into a cylinder, crammed it among other pieces of apparel in an already overloaded suitcase. "I'm ready, Gerry. I've got junk enough to last forever. Let's go."

Gerry got off the couch. He felt unbearably and suddenly homesick for all the other summers which would never return. "Take it easy, honey," he said. "I'll be back in about an hour."

"Gerry, what are you doing?" Jean cried after him as he started for the door.

"I've got to talk to Wallace."

"Why make a fool of yourself? You can't do a thing. You don't matter in this town, Gerry. Maybe nobody does."

He had not guessed the extent of his own stubbornness. He admitted, "I don't matter now. But two hundred years ago my family started this town. Orville Franklin built the first house in the county. He called it Green Hope."

Jean laughed. "Two hundred years is a long time to hope," she said. "When did the Mertons take over? Ten years later?"

He looked at her thoughtfully. "This is all ancient history, I know. But I ought to tell somebody I'm leaving. It ought to count, if the last Franklin walks out on the last Merton. If only to the restaurant owner."

Jean said resignedly, "You're crazy, Gerry. Who else but me would put up with you? You were in such an all-fired rush—now you'll keep me waiting for hours, maybe change your mind in the end."

She looked ageless and patient as a fertility goddess. Who had decided that Jean Moore was to be the town whore? When a town was dying, people were trapped in it beyond improvement—they could not grow or change.

Perhaps even Alice's hatefulness was part of the town's death throes.

Gerry returned to the house that was, he supposed, his legal residence.

The house would make a seemlier departure point from which to attend a town meeting than the good-natured one-woman brothel where Jean lived.

He was struck as he drove up by the intangible air of decay which clung to Alice's house as well as to Jean's, although Alice still had more than enough money with which to buy maintenance.

Men told the story of themselves, he thought, in the work of their hands as well as with their tongues. The local people who did Alice's gardening and house painting had managed, perhaps unconsciously, to tell of their broken spirits while working for Alice, if in no other way than the inaccuracy of a flower bed or the leaving off of half a pair of shutters after the painting was done.

The work of men who did not see a tomorrow—

Alice was out for the day, he found. She had not noticed his absence.

CHAPTER TWO

WALLACE BENTLEY was the third owner, as far back as Gerry's memory went, of the restaurant by the lake. Ten years ago, when there were more people, the place had been called The Palace and everyone rented it for wedding receptions or went there for dining and dancing. There had been a beach-level snack bar under the indoor dance floor, popular during the day with the younger crowd. You could lunch there on hot dogs, pop and ice cream, if you were sixteen or so, without changing from your wet swimsuit.

The younger crowd was gone, the name of the restaurant had changed, the activity had ended. At three in the afternoon, when Gerry parked in the clearing, the only other cars he saw were those which obviously belonged to Wallace Bentley and his handful of employees.

In the main dining room, tables had been pushed against the wall and chairs arranged in rows and aisles, obviously for tonight's meeting. Wallace was behind his bar, scowling at an open ledger book and clasping a tall glass filled with orange liquid. He was a handsome man, no longer young, with a trace of flair in the way he wore his houndstooth jacket.

He looked at Gerry with modified surprise. "Ah," he said. "A customer. The last of a dying breed. What can I fix you, Gerry? I'm sticking with orange juice myself."

"Make mine the same," Gerry said. The dimmed interior echoed. Damn it, as far as Gerry was concerned, this was still The Palace. Bentley had kept the building in good shape. Over there by that east window, Gerry thought, he had stood and watched the dancers the night of his high-school senior prom, wondering which girl to rush. In front of the musician's dais, he and Alice had performed a solo dance for guests after their wedding—one by one, the ushers had cut in according to time-honored practice—and where were the dancers now, who had come to the great wedding, the last expensive gesture that dying Oscar Merton would ever make for his daughter?

Ghosts. The years of the past, once separated sensibly from one another by landmarks, had run downhill together into memory's stagnant pond, to blend and to ferment.

The restaurateur poured orange juice for his guest, added shaved ice. Gerry sipped slowly, said, "I heard about your meeting on a radio broadcast. Think you'll have much turnout?"

"That's what I'd like to find out," Bentley answered. "Maybe no one in town gives a damn any more. In which case, I'll take my loss like a little man, let the bank take over the property and clear out myself."

"I give a damn," Gerry said.

"You?" Wallace's smile was not hostile, merely cynical. "You've got it made, brother. You can afford to watch the place turn back into forest. You and the little woman will keep on getting your cut whether Merton Mills are located in Merton or Timbuctoo. It's the working people and businessmen who have a problem."

"The area was a forest," Gerry pointed out, "when Orville Franklin found it. He turned it into a town."

Wallace Bentley sighed. "Save that stuff," he advised, "for the county historical society. Which, incidentally, used to have annual meetings here. They no longer do. The place has become too inconvenient and out-of-the-way." He paused. "I'll be serious. Hell, this is crisis. It's not only that the mill is closing—it's the reason the mill is closing. Roads. When the state voted the easterly route for the new highway, instead of having it come through Merton, we should have known we were licked."

"If you're so all-fired sure we're through," Gerry said, "why are you bothering to call a meeting?"

Bentley finished his orange juice. "A good question. I'll try to give you a fair answer. I'm calling a meeting mainly, I suppose, because I'm an American and Americans always call meetings. You can't feel a thing is real unless there's a public announcement to go with it, I suppose. Second, I promised a committee of leading citizens—which consists, I think, of me and Don Schaefer, the supermarket manager—that I'd explore channels and make a report. Third, I keep hoping like crazy." He turned his gaze from the darkly polished bar to the east window and the lake. "The place is beautiful. You can't make a living here, but you hate to leave. For some reason, I love it here and I'll miss it the rest of my life if I have to go away. You?"

"The same," Gerry admitted. "I love it here." His gaze followed Bentley's over the lake. "I tried to get away, one time. Finished college, the service, got myself a promising job in New York—I had to come back." He laughed mirthlessly. "Funny. You said you were submitting a report tonight?"

Bentley made a deprecating gesture with his handsome shoulders. "It isn't much. Just some suggestions from the state commerce department. For one thing, they recommended using the old brick mill for some other purpose, now that the Merton Corporation won't need it any more. A bakery, they thought. Sure, we've got lots of people in town who could work in a big bakery—but the problem doesn't change. If there are no trucking roads for bolts of cotton, there aren't any for bread. The railroad spur shut down two years ago. Another thought—if we can hold out another five years, they may build a new state college around here. On the other hand, they may not."

"I see," Gerry said.

"There's still one hope—but why should I tell you? What the hell, you're the enemy. Come to the meeting and let me hit you over the head with it."

"What do you mean I'm the enemy? What are you getting at?"

Bentley closed his ledger. "All right. I'll tell you. Our congressman feels Merton could be included in a state recreation area. Everything that makes the place hopeless for industry also makes it ideal for recreation. We're secluded. We're beautiful—scenically speaking, of course. We have facilities for swimming, boating, camping. City families could come here in the summer, rent cabins or pitch tents, take some fish out of our water and leave a few dollars behind to see us through the winter."

"It's a good plan," Gerry said. "Perfect, in fact. Why am I the enemy?"

"Are you kidding? Go ask Mrs. Franklin how she feels about peasants camping on the shores of Merton Lake. Take a look out there."

He indicated the world beyond the window with a sweep of his houndstooth arm. "A mile or so up the shore, you've got the Merton's lodge. Until old Oscar died, this was the most social shore west of the French Riviera. He'd have guests—and the guests brought guests. Business tycoons, politicians, theater people—it was business we could count on. Ferris, who runs the boats, used to take in thousands, just renting and servicing boats and guiding fisherman's parties."

"I remember," Gerry said.

"You remember like a kid. I remember like a businessman. The Mertons were snobs. Fair enough—snobbery is worth something in dollars and cents. You can sell it to other snobs. So we kept the public out of here—and the Merton crowd paid us to do it." He paused. "The public is still being kept out. The Merton Corporation may not keep the mill open here, but it sure as hell keeps a lobby active in the state capital—and that lobby's against any state park within a hundred miles of the town. I figure it's Mrs. Franklin's idea of privacy—but if that's the case, I wish she'd entertain like her old man used to do. By the trainload."

"I'll talk to her," Gerry promised. "We'll both come to the meeting tonight."

Wallace Bentley made a delicate snorting sound. Probably he knew—everybody knew—the extent of Gerry's influence over Alice Merton Franklin.

At dinner, Alice was charming, friendly. She had taken her car during the day, driven alone into the hills and found a spot to paint. She would have described herself as a Sunday painter, except that, as she had admitted in a moment of honesty, all her days were Sundays. She was an amateur at everything, even at love, Gerry thought. Perhaps that was the answer to the riddle of Alice.

He told her about his conversation with Bentley. "They blame you," he concluded, "for trying to kill the town."

Her beautiful face turned pale. She put down the fork with which she had been nibbling happily at a tossed salad. They were dining on the glass-walled patio which within a week or two would be converted to the screened-in patio. Just outside, fully visible in the evening light, a great magnolia bloomed to bursting with giant mauve flowers.

"That's totally unfair," she said. "You know it's unfair, don't you, Gerry? I have nothing to say about the way the Corporation is run. That's up to the board of directors. Why, I'm not even on first-name terms with them. Some of them are men who didn't know my dad. All that I amount to any more is a stockholder. Why should I be blamed because the mill is closing?"

"Because human nature is like that," he told her. "Someone is always blamed. I agree, though, that there's nothing you can do about it. How about this state-park idea? It was news to me. Have the Merton lawyers fought it?"

A stubborn secretive look came into her face. "I imagine they have. Once you let the government in, my daddy said, you've given away your life."

"But what's left for the people here? They have their homes and that's all. No jobs, no hope of jobs—"

She clasped her hands in a curious gesture compounded of imperiousness and pleading. "Let's go to the meeting, Gerry. Let's talk it over with everyone."

"I think we should," he agreed. "I'm glad you see it my way."

"I still don't like the idea," she said, her voice soft and sure, "of outsiders moving in. I don't want to live in a state park. It will make me feel like a species of wild life on the verge of extinction ... as though people from Brooklyn would have to be warned not to feed me."

She was beautiful. She was all the music in the world transformed into humanity and packaged as Alice. She was summer and sunset and joy. She was hollow. She was a painting of herself, done by an amateur hand.

"What would you suggest," Gerry asked, "as an alternative to a state park?"

"We—the town, that is—could go into the resort business ourselves, in a planned way. I don't mean impoverished gentility hanging out signs that say Tourists Welcome. I mean, go into business. I mean, let's all get rich again. I want to talk to the people, Gerry, even if they hate me. Maybe they won't hate me after tonight."

She had surprised him. "Lady," he said, "they'll love you."

An hour later they walked into Bentley's restaurant arm in arm. Earlier comers noted them. A murmur ran through the crowd.

Alice smiled at acquaintances. She squeezed Gerry's hand and whispered to him, the smile still bright on her face for all the strangers, "I'm scared. You were right—they hate me. Don't ever leave me, Gerry, no matter how bitchy I am. You're the only one who cares, now that daddy's gone. Everyone else in the world would like to see me dead."

They took their seats in the crowd.

Wallace Bentley presided from the dais. For a long time after the meeting opened, there was airing of already aired complaints, a restatement from one source after another of the town's hopeless position. These Wallace tolerated with an aplomb that Gerry admired.

Whatever conclusion was arrived at after the interminable talk, Gerry realized, the people would feel they had arrived at it themselves and perhaps they would be right. But first they had to unburden themselves once more.

Imperceptibly, the tone of the gathering grew more business-like. Wallace made his report. There was interested comment. The promise about the state college in another five years evoked laughter—and with the laughter, Merton seemed to become a community again.

Someone stood up and said, "Why couldn't this town make a business out of tourists?" The speaker was Gerry Franklin. He was surprised at himself.

A conspicuous silence greeted his suggestion. Don Schaefer, the supermarket manager, finally answered for the town. "You tell us that, Gerry. Or maybe Mrs. Franklin wants to tell us. We all want to know why we can't make a business out of tourists— why we can't have a state park here."

Alice raised a slender faintly suntanned hand.

Wallace looked at Gerry. "Will you yield the floor to the lady, Gerry?"

"I'll yield," Gerry said. But he was frightened for Alice when she rose to speak to these people who disliked her, who were jealous of her for being beautiful and wealthy and self-sufficient.

Her soft voice carried well. "I'm not very good at putting a point across," she apologized. "Please be patient with me. This is what I have in mind—a state park will limit us ever so much, establish government supervision of what we can or can't do. We'll be accountable for what we charge. We'll worry, as years go by, about changes of administration. We'll end by owning nothing—we'll all virtually be on civil service.

"Whereas if we plan to go into business privately—as a community—there's no ceiling on how much profit we can make. Am I making sense?"

"I think you're making terrific sense," Wallace Bentley told her.

Alice sat down.

Gerry breathed again. "Honey, you were wonderful," he whispered to Alice. "I don't know how you did it—but when you walked in here, everybody in town was ready to throw tomatoes. But now they're throwing roses."

She withdrew her hand from his. She was no longer frightened. The look she gave him was inscrutable and quiet, as though the real Alice were a million miles away.

Discussion continued. Alice's idea had caught fire and everyone had suggestions. Wallace Bentley was busy writing them all down. A vote was called for, to name an official organizer who would take care of raising funds, rebuilding, advertising. In a buoyant mood, people shouted their choices, ignoring parliamentary procedure.

"How about you, Wallace?" Don Schaefer called.

"Gerald Franklin," someone yelled. Curiously, more voices echoed the same name. Gerry was amazed. They liked him. Underlyingly, deeper than resentment, the town's feeling toward him was an amiable one. Why? Because he had come back when he might have stayed away—or for no special reason? He was profoundly moved.

If they trusted him with their project, he promised himself privately, he would see them through to success, come hell or high water. He must not let them down. From the comments about him, his choice seemed a foregone conclusion.

Wallace was rapping for order.

Alice stood up again. "Let's think with our heads," she said gently, "and not our high spirits. This is no job for an amateur. We need an expert, a professional, someone with experience in developing successful reports. No one in this town answers that description."

Gerry had an astounded sense of defeat and outrage.

They had taken a trip last summer, he and Alice, stopping at a dozen resorts, spending her money. On one stop they had met a self-made man of whom Alice disapproved. She had disapproved of him—volubly—after every horseback ride she took with him in the morning, every swim, every round of golf.

She had come back to Gerry and their suite to say, "I think Jack Chapin's as vulgar as they come. All he thinks of is making money."

"Then why do you keep having dates with him?" Gerry had replied.

"Dates? Good heavens, Gerry—don't call it that. It's just that you have to be civil to the other guests when you stop at a place like this."

Gerry had been glad when they moved on and she no longer had to be civil to Jack Chapin.

Tonight at the meeting, he remembered her impressions of Jack Chapin's vulgarity and hoped against hope that Alice had forgotten—that she was not about to say what he feared she would say.

His hopes proved groundless.

"Maybe you've heard of Jack Chapin," she went on. "He's rather famous for developing resorts. He could put us on the map. Maybe I could get him to come and help."

"Would he make us richer?" Don Schaefer soberly asked.

Alice answered the question with another question. "If you'd bought a piece of Miami Beach, say fifty years ago, for about ten or fifteen dollars, and you still owned it today, would you call yourself any richer?"

She had won, Gerry realized.

The town voted to have Alice get in touch with Chapin.

The meeting adjourned.

CHAPTER THREE

"STOP pacing," Alice ordered imperiously. "Pour yourself another drink and sit down."

Gerry kept pacing, not looking at her. He knew what she looked like. She was beautiful tonight—too beautiful.

And they were waiting for Chapin.

She was wearing a silver lamé sheath dress that ended at her knees. Diamonds sparkled at her throat and ears, making her an icily regal princess.

Icy or not, she was excited. She had not been excited at their wedding, Gerry recalled. She had been cool, poised, confident. He had been the nervous one.

Twin spots of color blazed high on her cheekbones. She had been a dynamo of housekeeping, getting the lodge ready for guests, driving Grace Troy and herself to exhaustion. Now the lodge was cleaned from top to bottom. New drapes hung at the windows that overlooked the lake. The drapes were silvery blue. They glittered in the light of the copper chandeliers.

Pacing in front of the windows, Gerry saw the lodge and its lights reflected in the lake. The image glistened, broke on a ripple, reformed over and over.

June had turned hot and humid. The water looked inviting. He wished he could jump in, fully dressed in his summer formals. The slightest of winds blew off the lake. Maybe the night would turn cool. Maybe a storm would bring rough refreshing gusts of rain and rolling drums of thunder.

Gerry had slept poorly since the night Alice had phoned Chapin and talked him into coming to Merton. Until tonight, he had hardly been able to grasp the fact that Chapin was really coming, that the world and its shapeless ugliness would move in on Merton. Whatever else Chapin accomplished, he managed to leave ugliness behind him.

"Gerry, there they are," Alice cried suddenly.

Gerry turned from the window to look at her. She was visibly stirred and jubilant. What did she expect from Chapin? What did she hope to get out of all this activity?

She knew Chapin's methods—he would take over. The local people would never know what hit them. Surely Alice could not hope to profit from turning Merton into a cheap wild resort town. Chapin would skim off the cream and everyone else, including Alice, would have to be satisfied with what he left.

She ran to the wide lodge doors and flung them open. Three long cars rolled up to the entrance. From the driver's seat of the first car, Jack Chapin stepped into the lighted doorway.

Though a man of medium size, Chapin gave an inevitable impression of vigor and bigness. In his mid-thirties, he looked boundlessly successful, a look he must have cultivated like an actor playing a part. Oddly, now that Chapin was present, Gerry felt better.

He had something to hit at.

"Well—well—Alice, my lovely darling." Chapin gave Alice a smacking kiss on the cheek. "What a gorgeous sight to welcome a man. Hi, there, Gerry."

Gerry gave his guest his hand, half expecting some referee to order them to their corners.

"Oh, Jack, it's so marvelous you could come," Alice enthused. Her cheeks flamed and her eyes sparkled. "I couldn't believe you were coming until I saw the cars."

"Could I disappoint a lovely lady like you?" Chapin countered gallantly. He put his arm about her waist, went up the steps of the lodge with her.

Behind them in the entrance, a slender blond-haired girl stepped out of Chapin's car. Gerry hurried to help her as she struggled with a vast portfolio.

"Here—let me." He took her case and set it on the steps. She looked at him out of clear blue eyes in a freckled smiling face. Her hair gleamed in the light over the doorway. "I'm Gerry Franklin," he announced. "Welcome to Merton." He had meant to speak conventionally. His words came out a sincere welcome.

"Thank you, Gerry Franklin. You're kind. My, what a trip. Jack drives like a madman."

"Jack is a marvelous driver. It isn't in Jack to do anything badly." The rebuke came from within the first car.

The blond girl turned to the speaker, who was struggling to emerge. "Let me help you, Teresa," she said. She reached for a heavy leather case.

Gerry took the case from her hands.

The other woman handed over three more cases, then unwound her own length and stretched her arms. She was middle-aged, black-haired, tall, with something brittle about her. "I'm Teresa Brent," she said, holding out her hand to Gerry.

"Gerry Franklin." Her hand felt feverish, nervous.

"Where are the servants?" she asked, staring around.

"They live in town." Gerry felt himself stiffen. "A man and his wife take care of the lodge, but they don't live here."

"Oh? You'd think that for once—"

A man and woman came from the second car, stretching and yawning. Their appearance was freakish, startling. Both mature, they had dyed their hair and their heads looked almost alike, both shining with patently false blond curls.

"Ted and Ann Short," said the first girl. "This is Gerry Franklin."

Ted shook hands limply. Ann gave Gerry a slow cool glance from head to foot that made him feel like a stud horse.

Another couple came from the third car, laughing, kidding each other. They were younger, more normal. "I thought you wouldn't make it, darling," the girl drawled. She told the others, "Bill can't drive as fast as Jack, yet he thinks he could be a racing driver."

"Come on in, kids," Jack called from inside the lodge. "The drinks are great."

"That's for me," Teresa said promptly. She went inside, leaving all her luggage on the steps.

Four of the others followed. The blond girl stayed behind. She picked up the portfolio and one of Teresa's cases. "I'll take these. Mind bringing a couple?"

"Don't mind at all," Gerry said. "What's your name? I didn't get it."

"I'm Louise Edwards, Jack's secretary." A scream of laughter came from the lodge. She winced. "You know this town, don't you? Is there a quiet place to stay? I believe in sleeping at night. But this crowd sleeps all day and carries on all night."

"We'll find a place. There's only one hotel and it's not too good. Maybe you could rent a cabin on the lake."

"Perfect," she said.

They carried the bags into the lodge, set them down.

Jack hurried to greet them, drink in hand, as though he had become the host. "Louise, honey, don't carry that stuff," he said. "Leave it to the servants."

"They live in town," Gerry said patiently. "I'll bring the stuff in."

"Yes, leave it to Gerry," Alice said, strolling over to join them. "He likes to make himself useful."

Gerry felt heat rising in his face. He and Alice could talk over that remark later, in private. He turned wordlessly and went back for more suitcases. Why did she want to humiliate him? Who else was looking out for her?

"I'll help," Jack said. "I haven't forgotten how to work." He put down his drink, hurried after Gerry.

On the steps he gathered a suitcase under his arm, picked up another in each hand. He said to Gerry, "Well, it's been quite a while since we last met."

"That's right."

Jack exuded vigor, size and good will. "Never thought you'd be sending for me. I thought you didn't approve of me."

"I don't," Gerry said.

"What's it to be? A fight to the finish?"

Gerry paused. He had no immediate plans but he was sure Alice would need him as an ally before this project ended. "We'll see," he told Chapin.

Alice appeared at the top of the steps. "What are you two talking about?" she asked concernedly.

"The weather, honey," Jack said. "Is it always this damned hot?"

"No, of course not. June is usually marvelous here." Alice was being defensive. "Tell him, Gerry. Tell him how it usually is."

"It's marvelous," Gerry said mockingly.

Jack flung back his handsome head and laughed aloud.

After they had carried the rest of the luggage indoors from the first car, Jack said, "Let the others bring their own. They're sturdy people. Dance all night, swim all day."

Gerry showed Louise Edwards her room. "Tomorrow I'll help you find another place to stay," he promised.

"I could fall asleep on my feet," she said. "What a day it's been."

"How long have you been traveling?"

"Since midnight last night. Nonstop."

"Good lord."

"That's the crowd," she said. "This mob functions best at fever pitch." She went to the window and lifted a drape. "Oh, what a beautiful view, Gerry—what a heavenly spot to live in. You're lucky."

He stood beside her, suddenly aware of her slender figure as a thing of beauty.

"This town would feel luckier," he said, "if we all found a way of making ourselves a living."

"How far does the water go?"

"The lake's about ten miles long and three miles wide. They have some decent cabins on the east shore. We could probably find one you could rent."

"Sold," Louise said. "I'd love it. Feel that breeze."

A jarring laugh came from below.

"These people," said Gerry. "Maybe I'm old-fashioned."

"Honey," she said briskly. "I know what you mean. And believe me, nobody who is normal feels that these animals are normal. They work hard, they play hard. They earn pots of money and they spend it."

"Who are they?" he asked. "Are they a company? Incorporated? Just what is the set-up?"

She kept looking at the lake. "Chapin finds people, picks them up, drops them. Right now he's working with Ted and Ann Short, who handle boats and docks and swimming pools, that sort of thing. Teresa Brent has been with Jack for years. She handles restaurants, bars, amusements. Bill and Patricia Rand are new. They handle housing—cabins, trailers, even shops."

"But this isn't a formal company?"

"No. It belongs to Jack and some friends. But he can throw them out any time. As long as they're in, they can dip into the till, be as wild as they please. Anything goes, if it makes money for Jack."

Gerry thought of the long-gone summers of his boyhood. "I was hoping," he said slowly, "that someone would develop Merton with intelligence, make it a good recreation area. Something the townspeople could be proud of." He had not expected to say that to anyone associated with Chapin. "I got outvoted."

She shook her head. "I've been with Jack three years now," she said. "I've seen the same thing happen over and over. We move in, we build fast, we rake in the first money. Then Jack sells out to the local people and leaves them to cope with problems— the shoddy tourists, the tough bars, the reputation. A few years later, the law usually moves in and closes down everything. By then the profit is gone. But Jack has had his, and he's long gone."

"And that's the way it always works? Jack and his shock troops start a town toward destruction, give it a kick, and let go?"

"I'm too cynical," Louise said. She turned away from the window. "Well, it's quite a life. Exciting. Thrilling. But I'm getting old. Do you think I could shut the door and get some sleep?"

"There's a lock," he said, getting the hint. "And I'm leaving. Good night, Louise."

"I'll see you tomorrow," she said. "I'd sure like to have a cabin all my own." Shrieks of laughter, a scream rang from the downstairs rooms. She winced elaborately. "A nice, quiet, peaceful cabin."

"I'll come about noon," he assured her. "I'll drive you around town, then show you some cabins that you might want to rent."

"Swell. Thanks a lot." She added, as he was about to close the door after him, "Gerry?"

"Yes?"

"Don't take it to heart. Learn not to care. It helps."

He smiled. "Let me know when you figure out how." He closed the door gently, puzzled by her presence and her association with this crowd of twentieth-century carpetbaggers.

He paused at the top of the stairs. Below in the main room of the lodge, Alice was sitting in a wing chair, glass in hand, the princess accepting entertainment. Ann Short and Bill Rand were dancing cheek to cheek. Jack was playing the old piano, hitting wrong notes, but hitting them with the gusto that probably passed for success at everything he tried. Teresa and Ted were standing at a window, talking rapidly, gesturing at the lake.

They were pitiful people in a way, Gerry realized—and dangerous. They could louse things up for the next two hundred years, out of nothing more than ignorance and greed.

Could he stop them?

CHAPTER FOUR

GERRY got to bed at five in the morning. He envied Louise, even if her sleep was made fitful by the raucous shrieks and laughter and the drums Ted had produced and insisted on pounding.

At least Louise was alone in the dark and lying down.

When they got home to bed, he was too keyed-up to sleep. He finally took a cold shower at seven in the morning, had breakfast and went downtown. He looked up several people who owned beach cabins, found two who were ready to rent them. Louise might like either one, he thought.

He wandered on familiar streets, had coffee at the corner diner, window-shopped at the hardware store. The display was dusty and pessimistic. No one was buying much in the way of tools these days.

At noon he drove out to the lodge. He wondered if he would have a long wait for Louise. As he slowed in front of the building she came through the door and ran down the steps.

"Good morning," she said radiantly. Her blond hair looked like honey in the sunlight. Her freckles, he thought, sparkled. "I thought you were going to stand me up. I heard everyone leaving about four-thirty or five."

"I couldn't sleep. I've found a couple of cabins." He heard himself—he sounded curt, unfriendly. He wondered if her radiant good humor, her evident healthy energy made him beat-up and cross by contrast.

She became quieter and remained that way as he drove along the lake shore. A bumpy side road led past the cabins that were, he had learned, for rent. The air was hot, close to windlessness, even near the lake.

"There's one cabin off by itself I think you may like best," he said. "We'll go there first."

"I'm afraid this is a lot of trouble for you," she said politely.

"No, not at all," he answered—but his tone seemed grudging, he was not sure why.

An unexpected bump in the road jolted them and Louise bounced in the air.

"Sorry," he said stiffly. "I should have taken one of the other cars. This one is mine," he explained haughtily. "The others belong to my wife."

"Oh," she said. The car was a mess, he thought. He had fishing tackle in the back that he had not cleaned since last fall. There was grit on the floor. The upholstery needed a brushing. He could not explain the relationship between Alice and himself to this healthy freckled girl who had probably never been deeply disappointed in her life.

Silently, they reached the south beach. Here the building of cabins had lagged. Rocks, shrubs and trees came to the water's edge, leaving no cleared beach.

The cabin he had in mind for Louise was two-story redwood. Dark pines hung over the roof, giving shelter from the midday sun. Two hundred yards of wooded space separated the cabin from the lake.

A motorboat rode the ripples, where a twisted dirt path ended.

"The folks who own this," Gerry explained, "have a house in town besides. Their kids are grown and don't live around here any more. They haven't bothered to open the place for the summer. They said if you want to rent, they'll come out and clean it up."

"It looks lovely," Louise said politely.

He was not sure she liked the place. He wanted her to like it, he realized.

They left his car and walked up to the cabin door.

The rooms smelled musty, but they were clean. How long was it—five years, ten?—since he had been in here. The furniture was yellow wicker, the kind most summer cottagers used, but not the furniture he remembered. A screened-in porch overlooked the lake. The porch had been added since Gerry's parents had sold the cabin when their brief spell of prosperity ended.

"It isn't fancy," he said.

"It looks comfortable." She poked the cushions on the porch divan. "Nice."

He showed her the downstairs kitchen, the upstairs bed-rooms. He repeated information he had been given. "Mrs. Stone said there are linens in the closets, but they need airing. She'll fix it up however you want."

"Nice," Louise repeated absently. She went to the windows, looked out at the lake. A canoe was drifting lazily in the sunlight. The canoeists were in blazing heat. Here shade and quiet gentled the day.

"This part of the lake is lonely," Gerry explained. "Your nearest neighbor will be almost a mile away on the east shore. Maybe you won't like that."

"I'll love it," Louise said. "Oh, this is perfect. When I'm through working at the lodge, I can come back here and rest. I won't even tell them where I'm staying." She gave him an inquisitive look. "Is the lodge your own summer place—yours and Mrs. Franklin's?"

"One of them," he answered. "My wife's father owned a good deal of real estate."

"This wasn't another of his places?"

His throat ached. "No," he said. "Another family built this cabin a long time ago." He volunteered further, "The man and his son did most of it with their own hands. Later they sold to the Stones."

"What a shame," Louise said. "I mean, to part with something you've built that way. Could I move in today?"

"I'm sure you could," he said. "Sure you don't want to look at the other places?"

She was sure.

He left the cabin reluctantly late in the afternoon. He would have been glad to stay and finish getting the motorboat in running order. Louise seemed to feel she had taken enough of his time, that for him to stay longer would be unseemly.

"Thanks ever so much, Gerry," she said as he left. "I'm afraid this was a lot of trouble for you, especially with the party tonight."

"Party?"

"Yes." She stared at him curiously. "Your wife has invited us all to a party at your house."

"Oh sure. The party," Gerry said.

Naturally there would be a party—most of the time there was a party. And his life function had dwindled to hosting Alice's parties. Tonight, though, he could kid himself that he was watching out for his wife's—and the town's—best interests by keeping an eye on a bunch of sharpies.

He was already kidding himself. What he really was looking forward to was seeing Louise again.

At home he found Alice preoccupied with preparations—dinner, drinks, ice, new records, flowers, caviar. She barely acknowledged his entrance.

He asked Grace Troy who was invited.

"Nobody from town, just Jack's friends," she told him. "Maybe Wallace Bentley is coming, but nobody else."

Alice was crazy, he thought, not to ask more of the towns-people to come and meet the entrepreneur who was going to put them all in the black. He felt like skipping the whole affair himself. He could duck out and spend the evening with Jean Moore.

But then he would not see Louise.

He dressed for the party in the same linen trousers and white jacket he had worn the night before.

Alice frowned when she saw him.

"If you would only bother to buy a new formal suit," she said.

"You look stunning and expensive enough for both of us," he retorted. Part of his mind marveled at his own unkindness. But he and Alice were always unkind to each other now.

She did look stunning in an ice-blue sheath of embroidered silk, with sapphires in her ears and at her throat.

He wondered what Louise would wear. Would she look like a million dollars—or would she look like Louise?

When she came, she looked like Louise. Her dress was print, with pink, blue and lilac flowers. Her bouffant skirt flared out when they danced. The neckline was modestly scooped and she wore a tiny silver pendant that rose and fell with her heartbeat. Her mouth was pink as the flowers on her dress. Absurdly, he wanted to kiss her.

Instead he remained the polite host, mixing drinks, seeing that everyone had enough ice, changing the records on the player. Once he wondered what more Oscar Merton could have done.

Wallace Bentley looked bored and a little angry. Most of these people were not only strangers to him, but obviously not his kind. Jack Chapin and Wallace got in a corner for about half an hour at one point, presumably to talk business. Wallace left at eleven, pleading the necessity of getting back to his restaurant.

By midnight, Gerry felt the party had turned senseless. Ann Short was drunk and hanging on Bill Rand's neck. Bill seemed too tolerant of this imposition to suit his wife, Patricia. Jack Chapin watched them all with cool, amused speculation.

Ann had another drink, turned sentimental and insisted on singing along with the records. Teresa Brent made overtly hostile remarks about people who could not hold their liquor.

Ted decided to console Patricia. They went outside, and did not return for an hour. When they came back, Patricia's dress was mussed, her hair was wildly disordered. There was sand in her hair, Gerry noticed. He winced.

By one o'clock, Louise was visibly exhausted, but kept dancing with Jack Chapin whenever he asked. She seemed to feel this was part of her job.

Bill finally deserted Ann for Alice. Gerry watched his wife, feeling a jealousy so stale that it had no shock value. He wondered how Alice would react to the handsome coarse young man.

Alice seemed fascinated by Bill. They danced cheek to cheek. Bill was hugging her boldly, his hand patting her hips.

Ann watched Bill with sodden eyes. She was lurching and muttering. Her unnaturally blond hair was in wisps around her face. Gerry asked Teresa to dance, feeling she had been alone long enough. He almost liked her for remaining aloof and disapproving while her associates came apart at the seams.

She was tall and graceful, not a bad dancer, surprisingly. She kept talking in crisp sarcastic asides.

"Look at that bitch," she said of Ann. "Can't hold a man more than a couple of years. You'd think she would give up."

Ann staggered over to Bill and Alice. She tried to pull them apart.

"Please don't," Alice said crisply, wrenching her arm away from Ann's grip.

"He wants to dance with me," Ann insisted. "C'mon, Bill. Let's dance."

"Go away, Ann," Bill told her. "I already danced with you." His eyes were merry as he watched the older woman. Her jealousy and desperation evidently amused him.

"C'mon, Bill. I won't be nice to you any more." Ann waved a glass recklessly. The liquor threatened to spill on Alice's beautiful dress. Bill swung Alice out of the way, turning his back to Ann.

Ann grabbed at his coat and pulled, letting her glass drop to the floor. She used both hands. Bill lost his balance. Ann pulled him to the floor, fell on top of him.

Alice drew hurriedly back.

She watched with wide startled eyes as Ann rolled herself against Bill and kissed him wildly.

"Hey, get up, you two," Jack ordered, starting toward them. "No rough stuff in public."

A change came over Alice as she watched the couple on the floor. Her lips parted in a faint smile. Her eyes were wide, not with horror but with a kind of sensuous pleasure at sight of the writhing bodies.

Patricia glanced at them over Ted's shoulder. Her arm grew tighter around the older man's neck.

Jack yanked Ann to her feet, held her back as Bill got up. Bill said nothing. He grabbed Ann's hand and dragged her to the door with him. They went out into the night.

"Well, what next?" Alice whispered, licking her mouth with a small red tongue. Her eyes were bright and dazed. She was enjoying this vicarious sex, Gerry realized. How crazy—his frigid wife enjoying the ugliest sexual impulses in others. She smiled as Jack caught her in his arms and began to dance with her.

Gerry felt revolted and helpless. He was accomplishing nothing, he jeered at himself—he was drifting, letting life eat him away, morsel by morsel, as it had eaten away Merton.

He saw Louise in the hallway.

"Leaving?" he asked, as she started for the front door.

"Back to my cabin," she said. "I've had enough."

"I'll take you home. If you don't mind my beat-up old car."

She smiled. "I don't mind at all. I thought I would have to walk. And in these shoes—" She wore needle-heeled pumps.

He did not drive directly to the cabin. Instead he took the long road around the lake. He wanted fresh air and was sure that she wanted it too.

They reached the cabin. "Shall I come in and make sure there aren't any ghosts?" he asked casually. He wanted to talk to her in this quiet familiar place, to forget the scenes of the evening.

"No, I'm awfully sleepy," she said. "Thanks for the nice drive." Her smile was still a wholesome thing in the freckled face. "I appreciate your finding the cabin for me, and bringing me home. I have a hunch the party will continue until morning."

"I wouldn't be surprised," he said. "Well—good night." He watched her go into the cabin of his boyhood summers. He had not told her what the place meant to him. Lights flicked on inside. He drove away reluctantly.

He hated the thought of going home.

The night was warm and he had a blanket in the car. He found a mossy remembered bank under the pines, pulled off his clothes and took a long swim in the cool quiet water.

Back on shore, he shook himself dry, curled up on the blanket and went to sleep.

He wondered how long this virgin shore would remain unsoiled, now that Jack Chapin had arrived to improve Merton.

CHAPTER FIVE

JACK CHAPIN had a restless image of himself. Sometimes he thought of himself as a kind of public servant, a Galahad of progress bringing employment and traffic to areas of economic stagnation.

Sometimes he felt amazed at his own shrewdness and ruthlessness. He was never bored with himself. He had never married. He told himself that he moved too fast to acquire family ties.

But secretly he had been searching for a woman, the right woman, a woman born just for him. She would have to be a lady to make up for his rougher side, yet a tough woman too, for he could not stand weaklings. She would have to be beautiful. He demanded beauty in women, cars and scenery. And finally she must be honest. He hated cheaters.

He had never given up searching for the woman, though he had often been disappointed.

Tonight he thought he had found her. Beautiful, mysterious, enigmatic, fascinating—Alice Merton Franklin.

He could not understand her, and that alone intrigued him. He enjoyed challenges and puzzles. Alice was a beautiful puzzle, a study in contradictions. She was wealthy, stunningly dressed, yet had few servants and seemed content to live in a small backwater town. She could have married excitingly, helped a man in any career—but she was faithful to local boy Gerald Franklin, who seemed to have good looks, some education and nothing else. She seemed immensely capable, yet she did not run a business.

Jack Chapin had been studying her all evening at her party. He had listened to the tone of her voice as she asked her husband to serve drinks. He had sensed her contempt and hostility for Gerry. Was she disappointed in her marriage? Ripe for a change?

Jack thought of Gerry Franklin as another puzzle, though not one in which he had great interest. It would be too easy to dismiss the man as a weakling.

There was an unknown quality about Gerry that made the entrepreneur cautious. Gerry did not work—he apparently lived off his wife—yet his neighbors in town still gave him respectful attention, something they did not seem to give Alice. There was a hidden strength in the man that he must discover, analyze and defeat, or perhaps be defeated himself.

Ted and Ann Short, Bill and Patricia Rand had become obnoxious to Jack by four o'clock. He was fed up with his gang. He had seen Louise and Gerry leave before two. Teresa was staggering with weariness.

Brusquely he sent them out of Alice's house and back to the lodge.

"You can finish your drinking there," he said, pushing them into their cars. "Get going. I'll be along later."

Rid of them, he returned to Alice.

She protested, "Why did you send them away? I loved the party."

"The party is not over," Jack told her with more assurance than he felt. He studied the beautiful face, the shadowed, mysterious dark eyes. "But I think we'll enjoy it more if there are just two of us. We haven't had a chance to get acquainted."

He watched for her reaction. If she froze, he would chat a while, then leave without making a pass. If she smiled, he would proceed.

She did neither. She stared at him, her face inscrutable. The sapphires glittered in her ears when she turned her head. The record player still offered insistent music for dancing.

He held his arms out toward her. She moved closer with languid indifferent grace. They danced around the polished floor of the big empty room.

His desire, never long dormant, came fully awake. He was stirred by the lithe body in his arms, felt a sudden heat from his chest to his loins. He drew her closer, one hand on her slender hips.

She stiffened. But she did not pull away.

"Alice," he murmured huskily. "You're so beautiful. You stop a man's breathing. Alice."

"What do you mean by beauty?" she asked. "Something to display? I've been on display all my life."

She spoke without coyness or vanity. His eyes narrowed. If she did not want admiration, what did she want? She was a woman of vast hunger, he sensed, but what was her desire?

As they danced, his hips ground against hers. She did not flinch.

He remembered her face as Ann and Bill had rolled on the floor.

Jack had never been subtle, though he admired subtlety in others.

"Alice, I want to make love to you," he said directly. "I want to show you what love can be."

"Love? Or sexual passion?" she asked. Her voice was cold but a flush was rising under the delicate make-up.

"They are mingled. One derives from the other." He tried to guide her to a wide couch. She stopped him.

"No. Upstairs. My bedroom," she said, as directly as he had spoken.

She had caught him off guard. His heart thumped raggedly as they went upstairs. She was going to give in to him, this proud aloof lady, this ice goddess, the woman for whom he had searched for half a lifetime. In minutes he would penetrate the mystery and possess all that she was.

In her bedroom, she closed and locked the outer door. She opened another door, glanced beyond at a second bedroom, an unmistakably masculine one.

"Your husband's room?" he asked.

Her smile told him nothing of what she felt. "Yes, his room. He isn't there. Your Louise is quite attractive and Gerry is fond of blondes."

She closed the connecting door. He felt suddenly sorry for her, an emotion that disturbed him. He admired the lift of her chin, the frankness of her replies. Had he found what was wrong between Alice and her husband? He hoped so. Unhappy, jealous wives were good partners in bed, he had found.

She moved to unzip the ice-blue sheath. He went toward her, turned her around, pulled the zipper down her back. His big hands drew the dress from her shoulders, down over the firm, high breasts, slim waist and lithe, sleek thighs. She stepped out of the dress, tidily went to hang it in her closet. He gazed at her figure as she moved. She wore only a strapless blue bra, blue panties, long stockings and silver shoes.

She took off her jewelry, laid it on the dresser. Hot and impatient, he pulled off his black bow tie and flung it toward a chair. He missed the chair and the tie hit the floor, but he did not try to retrieve it.

He ripped off his suit jacket and had torn off his clothes by the time Alice finished fussing at the dresser and walked daintily to her bed.

Her back was toward him. He unfastened her brassiere. The pink-budded breasts sprang free. She unfastened garters, and he pulled down the panties and stockings to her heels, examined her with quick, greedy glances.

She was more beautiful than he had dreamed. She bent to take off her slippers. The proud breasts brushed his cheek—the waist was made for his hands.

He pushed her back on the bed. She lay before him—ripe for his taking? Or was the mystery still hidden?

He bent over her, one arm under her shoulders, his free hand caressing her breasts.

Their first embrace was a blur of delight. Later he would remember her hesitation, her rigidity, her efforts to push him away. But tonight he would not be denied. He drove at her until she crumpled, accepted him helplessly.

Later, he bent over her once more, urged her to share his passion. The dark eyes were half-closed, watchful, suspicious. He forced himself to be patient and at last succeeded in rousing her.

The soft body writhed with desire. Her hands clawed at his back. Her breasts pushed upward at his chest—in an infinitely muted cry, she uttered his name.

"Jack—"

He smiled at her tenderly.

He brought her expertly to a peak of emotion. Alice fought him as she clung to him, her body helpless in the grip of passion.

He whispered, "Now you know what love can be."

Her dark eyes were lidded. She sighed with content.

He let her rest for moments, savoring what had happened to her, then roused her again with kisses. Jack had no moderation in him for anything he did—work, play, love. His appetites were enormous.

But Alice tired quickly. At last she pleaded, "No more, Jack. I can't—no more. Please."

When he left her, she was sleeping like a child. But no child had that heart-stopping figure or would be capable of that exciting response. He would teach her more the next time, he mused as he dressed.

He knew there would be a next time.

He was out of the house and driving his car toward the lake before he missed his bow tie.

Alice would find it and return it, he thought—or else Gerry would find it. That was the chance he took.

He felt a little disappointed in the session, he found. He tried to analyze his feelings. Had she been cold, or shy? Only at first. She had warmed overwhelmingly.

What was wrong with him? Was it his curse forever to be dissatisfied in possession of a beautiful woman? Was anticipation inevitably better than reality?

He laughed aloud at himself, admitting the answer he had not wanted to face.

He had thought Alice was a lady. She had given in to him, though, without a single struggle. She therefore was not a lady.

"You're doomed, man," he jeered aloud at himself. "When you get what you want, it's ashes. Ladies can love, feel passion. What's wrong with you? You ought to feel on top of the world. You've found the goddess of your dreams—and she came to your arms as though she had been dreaming, too."

He whistled as he reached the lodge. Everything was quiet— everyone inside was asleep at last. He showered, dressed, started to work, trying hard to forget his innate disappointment.

CHAPTER SIX

GERRY found Alice in a bad mood at lunch. "Where did you go last night?" she asked angrily. "What did you mean by walking out on my party? Where did you take that girl?"

Her fury baffled him, suggesting as it did some underlying fear. Usually she did not question what he did, as long as he did not interfere with her plans.

"I took her back to her cabin, had a swim and slept on the beach," he said patiently. He had had enough sleep to restore his good temper.

"That's hard to believe," she said stonily. Through most of the meal she remained unpleasantly disapproving.

Grace Troy, staring down at her plate, eating little, made no comment. Gerry felt sorry for Grace, was surprised at Alice's outburst.

Jack Chapin came by after lunch. "I'm borrowing your wife," he told Gerry cheerfully, "to show me around the area."

Gerry watched them leave, wondering if he should have tried to stop Alice. She was usually reserved and controlled with her guests but she had seemed nervous when Jack appeared.

He went upstairs, wandered about restlessly, telling himself that some day he would probably leave town after all with Jean Moore. He opened the door to Alice's bedroom, for no more reason than that the door was there and he had to keep moving.

Her bed was unmade and uncharacteristically messy. The sheets were pulled out from the foot of the bed, the blankets were on the floor. He frowned. When Alice slept alone, she usually left a bed almost the way it was before use.

Something on the floor caught his attention. He picked it up. A black formal bow tie.

Jack Chapin had been wearing a black bow tie last night. Jack had been here with Alice. And the bed had known violent use.

He was sick with shock. Remembering her nervousness at lunch, he supposed she had been a little sick herself.

He put the bow tie on her dresser where she could not fail to see it. What message he hoped to convey that way, he could not be sure.

Had she been drunk? What had Jack thought of her? Evidently he had stayed a long time. She must have shown him more passion than she ever had felt for Gerry.

He went back to his room, closed the door, sat down in a plush chair to think. The thoughts seemed to detach themselves from him, to become monsters that grinned at him from corners. Alice had never involved herself before with another man. What was Jack Chapin's attraction?

Maybe he reminded her of her father and her grandfather. They had been big piratical ugly men and maybe that was what Alice wanted in a man.

Jack Chapin could destroy her. Gerry wondered if he could save her—if he even wanted to try. What would happen to Merton in the meanwhile, to this beautiful back water town whose last remaining source of wealth was Alice's private income plus nature's incredible artistry? Would the town be seduced and ruined like Alice?

Gerry was not conscious of coming to a decision. During the afternoon at one point, he heard himself say to Grace Troy, "This time I mean it. I'm going away."

"You'll be back," she said. "You always come back."

"How can I come back now?" he asked.

She did not answer.

He had little sense of time or destination. Alice's infidelity had put him into a mental state where hours had no meaning. Without a drop of alcohol, he was in a condition like drunkenness.

He had flickering moments of astounded self-awareness, when the monstrous thoughts gave him an interval's peace during which to get his bearings. He seemed to be traveling through the state, having perfectly lucid appointments and interviews with people he knew, trying to promote Merton's potential.

One industrialist lost interest when he heard how small the town was. "Our people demand good grade and high schools before they will move. No, sorry, your town isn't for us."

A manufacturer wanted to hear more about the lake. He made boats and had considered opening a new plant. He qualified, "But we need highly skilled men. We can't move men who are already employed elsewhere. Can you supply two hundred workers?"

Gerry had to admit Merton could not. "You could train them, though. We have good men—"

The interview dwindled into vague assurances which Gerry knew were meaningless. A frenzy as quiet as a heartbeat—and as vital—kept him going. He was not sure where he slept. The days and nights were hot and ugly.

Down state, another man turned Gerry down when he heard where the town was located. "Too far from the big cities. Nope, our people wouldn't be interested."

A fourth man laughed gently at Gerry's eagerness. "Sorry, Franklin. Your town has nothing to offer. We're looking for a place near a university, where we could promote an outdoor stadium for sports or expositions. Merton would never do."

No one cared—no one wanted to bother with the town Gerry loved—except Jack Chapin.

The world felt like a bad place.

After ten days, Gerry gave up. More than his hit-or-miss efforts were required to find the industries Merton needed.

He pulled into town at nine o'clock on a clear summer night, decided to have dinner at the corner diner instead of going home.

He stared, pulling up to the curb to park.

The diner had changed. A huge neon sign above the door announced, "Joe's Diner," in flashing red and orange.

Gerry got out of his car and looked down the street. Another neon sign hung over Don Schaefer's supermarket but the featured attraction was far from hamburger or canned goods. MONTE CARLO NITE, the sign said ungrammatically. THREE TABLES. NO WAITING.

He murmured aloud, "They're kidding."

He heard a long low whistle, turned to see what was going on. Two plump women, wearing tighter-than-skin shorts, were wolf-whistling at Gerry.

"He's the best-looking thing I've seen in town," one of them said as she passed. She gave him a smile that was probably meant to smolder—a greasy smile, he thought.

Gerry entered the rejuvenated diner. Within, the jukebox was blaring. A man and woman were dancing. Gerry had never seen them before, which was unusual in Merton—as a rule, everyone knew everyone else. The strangers were loudly dressed, the man in shorts and open-necked shirt, the woman in shorts and halter. Where did they think they were—Tahiti?

And how had Joe acquired a liquor license in the week or so of Gerry's absence? There was a bar in the diner now, doing a brisk business.

And Joe was tending bar. Gerry walked over to him, asked, "What's going on?"

"How in hell would I know?" Joe countered. He looked flustered, rushed. "All I know is, I'm all of a sudden making money by doing what's suggested. But I wish I knew more about mixing drinks."

Someone yelled for Joe and he yelled back, "Coming."

Picking up a tray of drinks, he hurried over to a booth where six people were crammed in.

The entire mood of the place was transformed. Gerry no longer wanted to order a meal here. He walked out, wandered down the street as far as the movie theater and back again to the car.

Suddenly he wanted to go to the lake. At least the lake would not be changed, he thought.

The long stretch of beach was pale and bare in the moonlight. Here kids had gone swimming since the memory of the oldest inhabitant. Someone had put a fence around the area. A sign on a gate said, ADMISSION, $1. PAY AT THE BOOTH.

So now the kids had to pay to swim where they had been swimming for years as a natural right. Gerry drove past slowly. The beach was lighted and, though it was night, some people were in the water.

At Wallace Bentley's restaurant, the old Palace, he found the front entrance so crowded that he went around to the kitchen door. Wallace was in the kitchen. Gerry walked up to him, asked, "What's going on?"

Wallace turned from the supervision of a large dishwashing operation. The kitchen was crowded with workers. The chef seemed to have acquired an assistant and some local high school boys were at the sinks, looking lanky and out of place. Gerry wondered what kept them from throwing suds at each other in a friendly way—probably, he realized, only Wallace's watchful eye.

Sweat stained Wallace's shirt. "Gerry. What's new?" he said absently. He turned to his helpers again. "If you smash another plate I'll smash your face," he threatened.

The boys answered reassuringly, politely. "You bet, Mr. Bentley." They continued to hand the dishes back and forth between them as though they were passing a ball.

Wallace moaned softly and looked away.

"What happened? I was away ten days and look at the town—"

"Yeah. That Chapin is a fireball. I have customers like I haven't had in my life. Know something? I don't even like it. I went looking for you, to see if you could help me. But you were gone—you walked out on us. So if you don't like what you find, you can blame yourself."

Gerry did not answer. He looked through the kitchen door at the dining area. The place was jammed. Couples, packed like sardines, danced to the music of a mediocre band.

There were new murals, of a type never seen in the old Palace— mermaids, wearing little except their fishtails. Mermaids so poorly daubed that they could have only one purpose, to serve as a kind of suggestive joke. In crude suggestive poses under glimmering lights, the painted mermaids seemed visibly to gyrate and grind.

"How about that?" said Wallace, with a sort of meek pride. "Ever see anything like it before? Chapin's girl Teresa Brent contributed this masterpiece. She has another idea in the works—a live girl in a tank near the entrance, swimming around naked. The water will be mildly milky, not to keep us from being raided, but because it will be naughtier than plain nudity. I haven't got that fixed up yet."

"You're doing fine, Wallace," Gerry said slowly. "You're hustling."

"I know. Less than two weeks and the place is changing so I wouldn't know it." He sighed. "We asked for this, didn't we?"

"What's going on down the lake? Why is the beach fenced off? They're not going mermaid fishing, are they?"

"They're planning a dance pavilion. Room for a thousand people. No kidding. They'll have it ready in three more weeks."

Gerry felt new respect for Chapin, tinged with nameless dread. Jack really moved when he started. And in what direction was the town moving?

"I had to hire nine people," Wallace said. "Four men, five women. I need more waitresses. I can't use high-school girls any more, not unless they're over eighteen."

"I understand," Gerry said, still looking at the dining room.

A drunken male diner reached out for a waitress, wrapped his arm around her hips. The startled girl swerved and sat down on his lap with a plop. Her tray clattered to the floor. Wallace started toward her.

Gerry stayed in the kitchen where one of the boys made a sandwich for him, to take out. Gerry drove around the lake road until he found a quiet spot to eat his sandwich.

He had done his best and his best had been lousy.

Was it too late for Gerry to do anything for Merton? The town was on its way to a boom of business, brashness and cheap sex.

CHAPTER SEVEN

GERRY reached home close to midnight. He entered by the side door and went straight to his bedroom. Alice's room was dark and quiet. He slept uneasily. But when he woke, he was over the frenzy that had kept him traveling for days.

When he came downstairs Grace Troy told him, "Jean's been phoning you. She sounds about crazy. Wanted to know if you had left town for good."

"I'll get in touch with her," he said.

Grace had known Jean since childhood, was aware of the relationship between Gerry and Jean. She would never have betrayed them to Alice. She seemed not to like Alice too much. Gerry had never asked Grace to take messages from his mistress—she had done so unbidden. In some ways, Grace was more a mystery than Alice.

He went to the phone. "Hi, Jean," he said when she answered.

"Gerry—my God, I thought you'd left without me. Where have you been?"

"Out of town on business," he said.

"Please come right over. I've got to see you."

"I can't today, Jean. I'll come soon," he promised. He wanted to see his home town in daylight.

"Gerry, you've got to." She sounded near tears. "I almost went out of my mind when I heard you were gone. I thought I would never see you again."

"Now, Jean, you know better than that," he scolded her tenderly. "You know I wouldn't leave you without saying goodbye."

"Then come over. Please, Gerry?"

He felt like a heel, turning her down. "Well—okay. I'll come over. Fix me some lunch, Jean?"

"Sure I will," she promised joyously.

The part of town where Jean lived looked impervious to change. Certain kinds of decay, Gerry thought, had a pace all their own. They could not be hastened or slowed down.

Jean had made him a chicken salad. She hung over him and touched his hair and patted his shoulder.

"You're nervous," he said. "What's wrong?" He finished his coffee.

She sat and faced him. "I never thought I'd care about people changing this town—but I care. That gang your wife brought in— did you ever see such people in your life? Those two with blond hair in curls—honest, they scared me. I never saw such people."

"They're just posing, Jean—trying to be different."

"You can say that again." She plucked nervously at a napkin, folded it, unfolded it. "Gerry, I'm posing too. All the time—just to myself. I keep making believe I'm not a cheap tramp—and here in my home town, I get away with it because people are used to me. But what if things change? What if a lot of strangers come in?"

He said roughly, "Don't call yourself ugly names."

"That's what I mean. That's what anybody—well, almost any-body—would say to me in Merton. But others won't be polite."

"Polite?" he echoed. From Jean, the word seemed odd. After a second's reflection he realized why it would matter to her. A woman in Jean's profession would not hunger for love or com-panionship—but for courtesy.

"Why don't we get out? I've heard the folks talking. Lots of them are going to leave town if this new crowd takes over. They feel they'll be pushed aside. What will there be for you, Gerry? They'll laugh at you, strangers who are going to come. They'll call you bad names too, for not having a job, for living on Alice—"

"Will you shut up, Jean, please?"

"Why don't we leave now?" she persisted. "I'm afraid. I went to Joe's diner and men whistled. Men didn't use to whistle at me in this town, Gerry. Some wanted to bed me and they said so. But they didn't whistle first."

"What would we live on, Jean?"

"If we go somewhere else, you'll get a job."

"And what about you, Jean? What will you do somewhere else if men ask to bed you?"

She sighed comfortably, shifted her weight in her chair. The dining room where they sat was cool in spite of the day's heat, restful for all its shabbiness. Smiling, she patted his hand. "Now, Gerry, you know I don't bed other men, not any more. There was a time before you and I—but that's past."

"Sure, Jean. Sure. If it makes you happy, I'll promise to believe you. You're saving yourself for me. Right?"

"You know I am, honey," she said reproachfully. "And it isn't as though I didn't get other offers."

He rose and stood behind her, put his hands on her soft, plump breasts. "What do you say to other offers?" he teased.

"I always say no." She leaned back, covered his hands with hers, clasping them tighter against her breasts. "You know how I feel about you."

"Tell me." He kissed her hair, her soft cheek.

"I love you, Gerry. I love you an awful lot."

He lowered his face, breathed the fragrance of her hair. She was a big, shapely, comforting woman and yet she was far from enough to bring him peace. In this instant of quiet, his restless mind turned to his frigid and faithless wife.

His body was slowly roused to desire for Jean's plumpness.

But his emotions were still involved with the bitter mystery and the unfulfilled promise of Alice.

They went to Jean's bedroom. She undressed, stretched on the sheet and waited for him. He undressed and lay beside her.

She rolled into his arms with a satisfied exhalation, cuddled her generous curves into his limbs with the ease of long practice.

"Honey," she whispered. "It's been so long."

Their lips touched and caressed. She lay back, her eyes closed, her body weaving against his in a sensuous search for nearness. He was content for a long time to lie against her warmth and comfort, to kiss and caress, to touch her with hands and lips and limbs. Soon it was not enough for either of them only to touch.

Over and over the day's heat assailed the half-drawn venetian blinds and passed them by.

She held him closer.

Finished and satisfied, he drew away and lay beside her again. She snuggled like a lazy lioness, murmuring little pet names.

"Gerry?" she said presently.

"You want something, Jean. Out with it."

"If we don't leave town soon, Gerry, the town will leave us. There won't be any Merton—not the way we've known it."

He swore mildly. "Heads they win, tails we lose. Until now, Merton's been a dying town. Maybe more than dying—maybe the town was dead and we didn't know it—and we don't like what's coming after."

She echoed, "Dead—and nobody knew it. Like some people's marriages—like your marriage, Gerry?"

He silenced her swiftly in the only way that Jean could be silenced. They rolled across the sheets, drew out their long embrace the way they liked it. She was sweet and rough at the same time.

He remembered the time when Jean had first seduced him. He had been young and scared and curious. Jean had teased him into her bedroom, made him unfasten his belt and pull off his trousers. He wasn't a man yet, she had said, turning away with a pout.

Forgetting his guilty fears, he had pushed her across the bed and wrestled with her, trying to prove that he was a man. She had cooperated deftly and soon he had felt the soft unique shock of possessing a woman ...

The explosion of his own power had scared him and she had kissed and soothed and whispered to him until he was sure of himself again. A kind of pagan peace had come to his spirit. They had wrestled once more. When fulfillment came again, he had welcomed and rejoiced in it.

Jean had her own kind of virtue, he thought, drawing her closer in the warm afternoon laziness. The sun shone thinly around the drawn blinds and somewhere a screen door banged.

Gerry stayed until five in the afternoon.

When he went home, he saw Jack Chapin's car in the driveway.

He went in the side door again, oddly angry, and up the steps to his bedroom.

He took a long cold shower, dressed for dinner and went down to face the enemy.

Alice and Chapin were seated together on a couch near the windows. A tray of drinks was near enough to reach.

"Oh, there you are," Alice said. "I was afraid you wouldn't be home in time for dinner." But she did not sound afraid. She seemed rather sorry to see him.

CHAPTER EIGHT

CHAPIN raised his restless bulk from the couch as Gerry approached. His greeting was comparatively cordial. "Nice to have you back. Good trip?"

Gerry picked his tone carefully. "Not too good, not too bad." The men's eyes met. Chapin seemed amused.

Gerry poured himself a scotch, chose a chair that faced the couch and drank slowly. Dread had formed within him like a block of ice. The liquor warmed his stomach without melting the ice. Where was he heading? What would happen to him if he lost Alice? She liked Chapin as a person—that much was evident. The knowledge of her affair with the man was almost less alarming.

Alice's voice came through his thoughts. "Don't you think so, Gerry?"

"Sure. That's right." Gerry had not heard a word of the preceding conversation. Jack smiled at him, knowingly, winked. The wink was friendly.

Why did Chapin want to be friendly? Maybe he found it a challenge to seduce women and remain friends with their husbands. Maybe he liked everybody to be happy.

They went in to dinner. Gerry began to grasp that Alice and Chapin were discussing the progress of their resort plans. Alice was eager, enthusiastic, hanging on Chapin's every word.

Since when had the project become peculiarly theirs? Wallace Bentley had been the man who started the ball rolling on civic environment—Wallace was now forgotten in Alice's and Chapin's plans, their duet of heavy husky voice and positive soprano.

"—build along the south shore of the lake," Alice was saying with conviction when Gerry finally started paying attention to the words. "We could erect a series of cabins pretty cheaply, using the same design for every second cabin. They wouldn't have to be elaborate. They'll rent for a high price and—"

"And in a few years they'll be grimy shacks," said Gerry coldly. "The lake front will be a slum. But you and Jack won't care. Right, Chapin?"

Chapin's smile was slow to fade. "You don't like our plans much, do you?" he finally said in a mild voice.

"Don't pay attention to Gerry," Alice said hastily. "He's been drinking."

Gerry stated, "I have had one glass of scotch. I am probably much more sober than either of you. I asked Jack a question. He'll be long gone when Merton becomes a slum. Right?"

"I don't stay long in any resort," Chapin said. "Whether or not Merton will be a slum depends on the people who live here, not on me."

"But the people you plan to attract won't be staying long. They won't be the home-loving kind, will they? They'll be looking for a sanctuary for weekend sex, a quick hot time where nobody knows them. The kind who bring their families won't come to Merton. But others will come all through the summer, have a high old time, leave the beach a shambles, leave the homes a wreck, then leave. Right?"

"Gerry is hipped on the subject of a family resort," Alice explained to Chapin. "He doesn't realize how little money there is in families. He should, though. He comes from the oldest family in the county and he never has an extra penny in his pocket."

Somewhere nearby, Gerry knew, Grace Troy was listening whether or not she wanted to. Gerry began to have an uncomfortable feeling—though he fought it—of being in the wrong.

"You're accusing me of corrupting Merton," Chapin said. He waved Alice's objections aside with a gesture when she tried to silence him. "No, let me talk, Alice. You're accusing me, Franklin, of leading your lovely town down the primrose path.

"Let me tell you something. Nobody corrupts a town that doesn't want corruption. Nobody builds a fast tough money-making resort out of a town unless the citizens want money more than a decent life for their kids. Maybe I speed the process. I'm a fast guy. But your Merton would have gone this way sooner or later. The folks here want cash and they don't care how they get it."

"That's a lie," Gerry said hotly. "The folks here don't know what they're getting into. They've worked in factories all their lives and they suddenly have no work. If someone tells them they can make a living by turning Merton into a resort town, all they know is they need to make a living for their families. They don't know where they're heading. If I tried to tell them what you're up to they wouldn't believe me."

"Why should they believe you?" Alice asked coldly. "They know you. You married for money. Why should they believe any-thing you say about making a living? You're a good one to talk."

Gerry turned on her. "You've gotten me fired from every job I could have had in Merton. I'd be working right now if it weren't for you."

"Please, friends," Chapin interrupted, his tone half-humor-ous, underlyingly uncomfortable. "Save your quarrels for your bedroom, for my sake." He turned to Alice. "Suppose we discuss the weather. Or would that bring on another quarrel?"

Gerry realized he was the host here. He had been rude to a guest in his own house. He became unhappily silent.

Jack Chapin left immediately after dinner. Alice turned on Gerry furiously.

As soon as they were alone, Alice asked Gerry in a shocked voice, "How could you be so rude—and so stupid? Are you trying to drive away the only man who can help us make a living?"

"Yes," Gerry said. "Exactly, precisely. I am trying to drive him away."

She said, "I could kill you." Her fists were clenched, her eyes sparkling with fury. She looked vibrant with rage—and more beautiful than ever. "The town trusted me to find Jack and enlist his help. Why do you make it so hard for me? Jealous?"

"Of you? No. I'm sorry for you. But you're a thick-skulled mean-tempered gorgeous little birdbrain. You're—"

"Oh, Gerry." She came toward him in an abrupt change of mood and put her hands on his shoulders. "Gerry, what's wrong between us?"

He felt himself weakening, ready to agree with her on anything. It wasn't often these days that Alice bothered to be charming to him. He looked away. "You tell me," he said stiffly.

She murmured. "I hate it when we quarrel. We've been like this ever since the mill closed. You know something has to be done. I can't live with people hating me. My father did—but he was stronger than I am."

"We don't agree on what must be done."

"I realize that you're worried about what will become of the town, darling, and I admire you for that. But try my way, won't you? If you do, I'm sure things will work out better than if we fight each other. People will have jobs again. You'll have a job too. You'll have a big job."

"Sure I will," he jeered. It crossed his mind that both of them had been faithless to this marriage. If people betrayed a marriage, could they be trusted with the welfare of a community?

She put both arms around his neck, pressed her slender body against him. "We've lost our way," she murmured, as though she were reading his thoughts. "Just like our town. But the town is coming back. Look at the business Wallace Bentley is doing. He never had this kind of business before. Others will make the kind of money they only dreamed about before. I was right not to let them go through with a state park. Just wait and see, Gerry. Help me, don't hinder. I need your help, Gerry."

He knew what she was doing to him. Her talk, her caresses, the pressure of her body were seducing him from any convictions he held. But he could not resist her. He had never been able to do that. He hugged her fiercely.

They went up to her room, that mysterious place of suffering and delight for Gerry. He went to bed with her, joined in her willingness to be loved. He forgot Jean, forgot Chapin.

She was so beautiful, he thought, bending above her in the moonlight that streamed across her bed. Her face was in shadow under the dark hair, her eyes half-closed.

For the first time, her mouth was warm and passionate. He kissed her over and over, dazed with joy. This was the answer to all sorrow. Her sweet, warm mouth, her arms—he felt he could do any task, meet any challenge.

His hands touched her proud, hard breasts. They quivered under his fingers. Tonight she was willing, eager—he must have been demented to think she cared for Jack Chapin. Tonight must be a turning point in their lives—why, he did not know.

He knew only that at last his wife seemed to love him. He caressed the slender hips and strong, slender thighs. He kissed her all over. She did not stop him. She was moaning a little, her lips parted.

From some deep erotic lull in herself, she murmured a name. "Jack—"

Gerry died, came to life again a lesser man.

Jack had been teaching her passion—that was why she had changed. Jack Chapin had been with his wife. Alice was lost to Gerry forever.

Desire drained from his body. He rose from her bed.

She opened her eyes. "Gerry—honey? Where are you going?"

"To my own bed," he said. "I guess I'm tired tonight."

"Oh, Gerry," she said angrily, sitting up. "How can you leave me now?"

"You'd be surprised," he told her. "You're lucky I'm an ineffectual sort of guy. Otherwise I might kill you."

He went to his room.

For a long time he lay in the dark, incapable of thought but not of pain.

CHAPTER NINE

BY mid-July Jack Chapin knew that Alice was an obsession with him. It had ceased to be enough for him to rouse her passion and to satisfy his own. He thought of her constantly, wanted to know all that he could about her. He had many excuses to see her, of course.

By some pseudo-official self-determination, they were supposed to be working together on the resort project. During the dry sunny summer days they made tremendous progress. The dance pavilion on the lake was completed in record time. Alice's plan for a string of look-alike lakefront cottages would become reality in time for this year's Labor Day trade.

She showed tremendous interest and aptitude. Jack began making a few secret plans of his own. Alice could get rid of her husband. Jack and Alice could be married, work together all the rest of their lives. Alice was not quite the woman of his dreams—but he no longer wanted another dream woman.

Deep-seated caution kept him from confiding his plans to Alice. Life, he had found, could be rough on hopeful people.

He had not meant to discuss her with anyone. But one afternoon at Wallace Bentley's restaurant, he found himself drifting helplessly into conversation about Alice and her family.

"What were the Mertons like?" he asked Wallace. "Rumor says they were tough. What kind of tough?"

Wallace looked up from the blueprints on his bar, which he had been studying. His pencil point still hovered over the diagram.

"Tough? Depends on what you mean by the word. Before my time, old Ben came here from somewhere else, maybe Europe—no one is clear on that. This town was founded by the Franklins, Gerry's folks. Ben Merton came and took over. He started the textile mill and ran everything. He even changed the name of the town from Green Hope to Merton."

"An egoist." Jack felt he had learned something about Alice rather than about her grandfather. Not that Alice would be exactly like the old man. Far from it. She would reflect, however, a chain of spiritual cause and effect that derived from past generations. "How did he get control? Loan folks money?"

"So I've heard. And his son Oscar kept the system going. Oscar was slicker than his dad, not so obvious, you might say. If he heard about someone in trouble, Oscar would go to the man and offer to help. All you had to do was vote for the sheriff he wanted and the laws he wanted. Too bad Oscar didn't have a son. It was the only thing he ever wanted that he didn't get."

"What kind of woman did he marry?"

"Her name was Serena Gray. They met in college, I heard. She died about ten years ago, a year or so after I first came to Merton. Alice was still a kid at the time. People felt sorry for Alice for losing her mother so young. Funny thing, though—people are never very kind to the rich, sorry for them or not."

"This Grace Troy, this housekeeper—was that when she came into the picture?"

"I guess so. I had my own business to tend to—I wouldn't have noticed Oscar Merton's household problems."

"And Serena, Alice's mother—what was she like?"

Bentley smiled. "She was lovely. By the time I knew her, she was no longer a well woman. Other people say she was beautiful before she got sick. A nice person. Quiet." He turned back to his blueprints. "And now I'd better start minding my own business—which is supposed to be your business too, by the way."

"Oh, sure," Chapin agreed.

When Jack went to see Alice that afternoon, he found himself studying her with a more informed curiosity. What was she really like inside? A grief-stricken teenager, braving the world without her mother? Or did her ever-present reserve hide a will of steel like her father's and grandfather's? Had her father made her feel unwelcome because she had been a girl? More than any of his previous mistresses, Alice moved Jack to ponder the tragic glory of being human.

Her husband was absent much of the time. Alice seemed neither pleased nor displeased. She would merely say, her voice hardened a little, "Gerry is gone again, who knows where? Will you mix some drinks for us, darling?"

Jack mixed drinks. They talked. He was alarmed by something in her tone. "You don't want to pour a lot of money into cottages," he told her warningly. "Keep your plans within limits."

"Why? If you want to make money, you have to spend money. Father used to say that." Her lovely oval face was flushed, her eyes sparkling. She sipped her martini like a thirsty butterfly. He had a sudden uneasy feeling that she might, without knowing it, be a compulsive gambler.

He wondered if he should warn her, or let her go crashing to her own destruction. He decided to compromise. "Look, Alice. In these resorts you sometimes have to make do with what you have. You put money where it's necessary to convert a place into a tourist attraction. But if you build too big, you may get stuck."

"You never get stuck, do you, Jack?" She said it so mildly that he smiled. She was not innocent about money. "You make your quick profit and then you pull out."

"You've got the idea." He tapped the plans that were spread before her. "Something like this, you won't get your money back for five years. Will the resort last that long? You have to figure on human nature. People go for fads. They like a place one year, the second year it's all the rage to go there, the third year it's done."

"You think that will happen to Merton?"

"Who can tell? I stay long enough to give a resort a good start, then I let others take over. I get bored if I stick around anywhere too long."

She looked again at the plans. He wondered a little uneasily what thoughts were going through her head. The specifications she had developed were for something far more permanent than his own hit-and-run operations called for. Her decision could be important.

She surprised him. When he sat down beside her on the couch, she said, "What about women, Jack? Do women bore you quickly? Do I already bore you?"

Most women bored him as quickly as a single work project did. He did not want to tell her so. Feasting his eyes on her slim beauty in the shirt and brief linen shorts she wore, he put his hand brazenly on her bare, tanned knee.

"You don't bore me, baby," he said softly. "When I make love to you, I forget everything else in the world. When I leave you, I can't wait to come back. When I see you, I can't wait to make love to you again."

A smile hovered on her lips. She lowered her eyes demurely. He put his arms around her demandingly. He had to lift her face to his. Her lips were cool when he kissed her.

Each time he had to court her all over again. Each time she was an ice queen to be melted before she turned human in his arms. Was that part of her mystery? Was that why he kept coming back again and again?

Impatiently, he pushed her back on the couch. His hands went to the belt of her shorts. She clasped his hands and stopped him.

"Not here, Jack. I've told you that. Only in my bedroom."

He sighed and stood up. If only once she would forget all conventions and let him take her instantly at the moment of swift desire, he would have been totally happy with her. But she never forgot herself or where she was. She always observed the surface rules of convention. Why? Innately she was reckless rather than cautious, he was sure.

They went upstairs. The hot July sun blazed into her bedroom. Alice went to the open windows and pulled the blinds so the room was shadowed. The air was still warm and humid. If Alice had been another kind of woman, Jack would have suggested going to the lake, making love in the shade of the pine trees along the shore. But Alice would never do anything like that. Someone might see her.

He forgot his frustration when she took off the shirt and shorts. He stared hungrily at the slim, white torso, the tanned arms and legs. She stretched sensuously on her bed as he undressed.

He stopped wondering what she was thinking, what went on behind her enigmatic eyes. Right now she was outstretched before him. Later he would have time for puzzles.

He sat beside her. His trembling fingers fondled a breast so exquisite it might have been a model for a marble goddess. He bent to kiss her breast, felt the tensing of her body. Why did she brace herself for his kisses? He was not rough with Alice—he tried to be gentle each time.

He lay beside her, moved his arm under her shoulders.

"Honey," he murmured, using the words that would soften her resistance. "Sweetheart. My beautiful."

His big palms smoothed the resilient flesh. He kissed her neck and shoulders. She tasted of honey and perfume. Her fragrance dazed him. He turned rougher in his desire, crushed her closer. He pressed against her, trying to arouse her. She was ivory, cool and hard ...

Finally the tautness went out of her. She sighed. Her arms went around his neck.

He tried to be gentle, but he had waited too long. His desire was a hot fury for possession.

She moaned, holding his head in her hands. Her hips shuddered in a frantic effort to evade him. She must not get away. He had to have her. It was as though he were nailing their very souls together. She cried out, then stopped fighting him while he overwhelmed her with wave after wave of passion.

The second time, she was ready and willing. Deliberately, he protracted the gesture of love. He kissed her all over her white, enticing body. This time, in their union, he felt her ecstasy blossom.

They spent the rest of the afternoon in bed. He had the satisfaction of one embrace in which she lost all control over herself. She clung to him and begged passionately, "Jack—sweetheart—stay with me, please—"

There was passion in her, though it lay deep and was hard to awake. But it was worth all the trouble and time, to see the eyes tight shut, the face pale with effort, the lithe body leap to meet him. She could be beautiful in a different way, not only like an ivory statuette, an ice queen. She could be a woman, trembling with desire and ecstasy, taut with strain and yearning for fulfillment. All mystery could be consumed in one overwhelming surge toward union.

Jack Chapin felt wonderful that night as he left Alice's house. She was learning love from him, learning what a woman could mean to a man—and a man to a woman. She still had repressions to overcome. But one day, she would be a woman to worship and adore, the woman he had been seeking all his life.

And he would have fashioned her himself, not out of clay but out of ivory and ice.

In a life of transitory effort, she would be his one lasting achievement.

CHAPTER TEN

EACH July night was a little longer, a little hotter, than the one which preceded it. Gerry found in himself a strange indifference to life. He watched Merton change from a sleepy small industry town into a brassy tourist trap. He watched his wife Alice sparkling like an imitation diamond whenever she came near the developer Jack Chapin. He watched his friends and neighbors caught up in money fever, pouring funds they did not own into restaurants and tourist homes and beach attractions which they hoped would pay off.

Gerry was the silent onlooker, shrugging when asked for an opinion. They were all riding hellbent for destruction. Why spoil their fun with his gloomy warnings? He knew they would not listen in any case.

He spent all day and much of the night on the lake. He paddled his ancient canoe, grimly avoiding the drunken tourists in speedboats whose motors drowned out bird songs. When his favorite stretch of beach was roped off and excavations started for houses, he moved to another area.

He hoped that the boom would end in bust before the whole lake was surrounded by shacks, restaurants, soft-and hard-drink stands. Maybe the bust would not come in time to save either the lake or the town. Then what? There seemed nothing he could do about it.

Some dark compulsion forced him to remain and watch disaster. He felt that his wife was a moth fluttering nearer and nearer to Jack Chapin and his destructive crew. He was disgusted to see her attracted also to Ted Short, the limp light-haired middle-aged concessionaire who seemed to Gerry the epitome of decay. He could understand her attraction for Jack but not what she could see in Ted Short. For the first time, Alice made him shudder in distaste.

He stayed away from the gang that clustered around Chapin. He had not disliked Louise Edwards, but somehow nothing mattered during those July weeks. He wanted to see no one, talk with no one. He wandered like a ghost haunting a dead civilization. Sometimes he was surprised that anyone could see him.

Tourists, a hard-drinking crowd, had filled the local hotel.

All the beach cottages were taken, and more were being built by Merton Enterprises, composed of Alice and Jack Chapin.

One evening, tents were set up on the beaches, tenanted by strange-looking women. Gerry gathered that they were camp followers, like the prostitutes who followed soldiers, in warfare, available to anyone.

All-night beach parties became standard. Gerry, sleeping in a blanket, would wake to see fires lighted on the shore and couples dancing around them like mad primitives. He would hear shrieks of laughter, snatches of music, drums beating, drunken tormented screams. It was like trying to get to sleep on the edge of hell.

He rarely went home. Alice barely spoke to him on the rare occasions when he appeared. Grace Troy kept him supplied with provisions and washed his clothes. The Chapin crowd was always in and out. Gerry wanted nothing to do with them. Chapin eyed him curiously when they met, but said little.

One night Gerry was roused by two women who wanted to be "friendly." He rolled up his blankets, packed his pans and food in his car. He drove up and down the beach, looking for a quiet place to sleep, but none was left.

This was the ultimate cutting off of sanctuary. Roused from his lethargy, angry, he kept driving on the shore road.

Someone called his name from a lighted cabin door. He braked to a stop. Louise Edwards was waving to him from her screened-in porch.

"Hi," he called back. "You look comfortable."

"I'm extremely comfortable. Where have you been? I haven't seen you for ages."

On impulse he got out of the car, walked toward her porch. "I've been wandering around," he said, "watching your boss' work."

She opened the door. "Come on in." She continued, as he stepped inside, "I do love this house. I'm so glad you found it for me. It's been a refuge."

"From the looks of Merton these days, you need a refuge."

She grimaced. "I've never seen such a noisy town, night or day."

"Chapin ought to be real proud."

She was studying his face. "Have you had dinner? In fact, have you eaten this month? You're terribly thin."

"Haven't felt much like eating. Too hot."

"You sit down. I'll bring something."

He lacked the will to protest. He took a wicker chair facing the lake. The moon had risen and a path of shimmering light raced along the water. The scene would have been beautiful, except for the zigzagging headlights of the boats, reminding him of the rape of the lake he loved.

Soon Louise brought him a tray of hot food. He protested. "I can't eat all that. You shouldn't have bothered."

"I haven't eaten either. Pull up your chair. It's good to have company, someone nice to talk to."

She was so cheerful and matter-of-fact that he felt ashamed of his melancholy. He let her coax him into eating a full meal, complete with hot coffee.

He felt better after dinner. He knew he had eaten poorly in recent weeks.

"You haven't been much in evidence," Louise said. She opened a pack of cigarettes, offered him one. He lit hers, then his. She leaned back, exhaled lazily. "Chapin's been wondering what you were up to."

"That's his worry."

"You act like a bear with a sore foot." Her smile took the sting from the frank words. "If you don't like it here, why don't you leave Merton? You could get a job somewhere else, couldn't you?"

"I will eventually. I want to stick around a while and watch the walls fall down."

"I see." She finished her cigarette, stubbed out the butt. "More coffee?"

"No, thanks."

"What did you expect, Gerry? This town was dying anyway. The textile mill had closed. People were leaving. At least this boom will help them leave a little more comfortably. When the walls fall down, as you put it, that will be the only difference."

"It could have been different," he said. He leaned against a cushion, twining his fingers behind his head. "It could have been quite different. Wallace Bentley and I talked it over once. We could have made this area a family resort. We thought about letting them build a state park, attracting families with kids, the same families each summer. Things have moved too fast. We could have made this a good resort, with a long-time business. The fishing is good from March on, you know. Or used to be. By now, the boats have ruined the fishing."

Campfires were appearing in the velvet dark, all around the lake. The drinking, the screams and the laughter had begun.

"You really think your plan would have worked? You really think there's a living in family resorts?" Louise asked with kindly scepticism.

"Sure there is," he said tiredly. "There are always ads in the paper, families wanting places to go for a couple of weeks, where they can take the kids."

"I wouldn't know much about families," Louise said. "After my folks got a divorce, my mother remarried. Her new husband hated kids. Pretty soon he hated my mother too. So she got herself another husband."

"I'm sorry."

Her face was in shadow. He could not make out her expression.

"Well, that's beside the point," she went on presently. "Chapin thinks a family resort wouldn't pay. And your wife is sure of it."

"How many family resorts have they built?"

"None," she admitted, laughing. "You are persistent, aren't you?"

"We both know that this resort won't last more than two or three years. I saw some women on the beach the other day who—well, the county will have to crack down pretty soon, if not this summer, then next summer. We've already had two bad automobile accidents from drunken drivers. How long will it be before neighboring communities realize that quiet old Merton isn't quiet any more?"

"I'm sorry, Gerry. I suppose you're right. This state is pretty strict. Let's hope Merton lasts at least a couple of summers—enough for some old-timers to get back their investments."

He was silent, gazing out at a scene that was his no longer. He felt as though he were sitting at the deathbed of a friend.

"Gerry," Louise interrupted his thoughts, "where have you been sleeping nights?"

"On the beach."

"It's getting pretty crowded."

"Right."

"You could sleep in front of my house tonight, if you like. Nobody comes near, at least not yet."

"Thanks," he said. "I believe I'll take you up on that."

"Or else you could sleep in one of the bedrooms here."

"No, thanks. I'd rather sleep outdoors."

"I wish you didn't care so much," she burst out. "I wish you weren't such a nice guy. Why don't you leave town? Why don't you get out before they cut you to pieces?"

He moved to the wicker couch, sat beside her. "What does it matter to you?"

"It matters."

He touched her cheek, found it wet with tears. "Your heart is too soft, Louise," he said. "You shouldn't care either."

She moved into his arms. He kissed her mouth blindly in the shadows. Her lips were soft and parted. Her kiss turned savage, hungry. He sensed a loneliness in her that was deeper than his own.

They went outdoors to the beach, spread blankets under the pine trees. Without shame or protest, Louise took off her clothes and folded them aside.

He undressed and lay beside her on the blankets. She was sweet in his arms, clinging to him silently.

For an hour in the night, he learned, a man and woman could make the illusion of a world. An unspoiled private world ...

Her body clung to his. Her fingers dug into his flesh.

She was receptive and gentle as he possessed her, as the lake waters had been in summers past. The wind blew above them, cooling their hot bodies. Without knowing when sleep came, arms around one another, they fell asleep.

Gerry awoke during the night and drew a blanket over them. In sleep, she cuddled closer. He caressed her until she awoke and wanted him again.

This was better than being alone in the night. But the loneliness tomorrow would be much worse.

Toward dawn Louise said she was cold.

"I'd better go inside, Gerry," she told him sleepily "I'm not used to this outdoor life."

"Yes, go on in," he said.

"I'll see you tomorrow, maybe?"

"Maybe," he said.

She went into her cabin, trailing a blanket and carrying her clothes. He watched her go. He was wide awake, restless, impatient. Could he have done more for Merton? Was there something that he still could do in the face of Chapin's big plans?

He gathered up his clothes and his blanket, packed them into his car and started for home.

He crept into his silent house like a thief. It was five in the morning. He went to his bedroom.

He frowned, looked at the closed door that led to Alice's room. Was her radio on? He heard a man's voice, deep and husky.

Then he heard Alice's voice.

She was saying, "Jack. Honey. Don't—no more—"

"Once more, sweetheart." The male voice carried assurance. "Once more—my darling—my lovely—"

The voice was unmistakably Jack Chapin's.

Gerry ran blindly out of the room and down the stairs. He paused long enough to pick up several bottles of scotch. Cradling them awkwardly in his arms, he stumbled out to his old sedan. He dumped the bottles on the seat beside him and started to drive.

He parked somewhere on the lake road and drank himself into a stupor, jolting down the raw liquor as fast as he could absorb it. He had to forget the sounds he had heard from Alice's room. It was one thing to guess she was unfaithful—quite another to know, to be absolutely certain, to be a witness to her unfaithfulness.

CHAPTER ELEVEN

WHEN Gerry awoke the sun was blazing against his windshield. He felt as though his eyeballs were on fire. He groaned and a thousand hammers echoed in his skull. His hangover made his stomach a thing of horror.

He rubbed the back of his neck, wishing he were dead. Unfortunately, he seemed to be alive.

He drove aimlessly, stopped when he came to Wallace Bentley's restaurant. Good old Wally would give him something to kill this headache with—or to kill Gerry himself, whichever happened first.

Wallace was in his office, figuring accounts. He looked up. "Gerry Franklin. My God, you look horrible."

"Hungover. You have anything?"

Wallace grunted, got up and went to his kitchen. He returned with a mixture of tomato juice and clabbered milk which tasted as foul as it looked. Gerry downed the concoction, gagged over it. "What's in that?" he asked. "Poison?"

"You're the one who has poison in you." Bentley's shrewd eyes surveyed Gerry thoughtfully. "Where have you been? On a binge?"

"Something like that," Gerry admitted. He sat, bent over and breathing hard, in Bentley's spare office chair. The cooks in the kitchen were all too busy. Gerry tried to ignore the aroma of food. But soon he began to feel better. The pink hideous tonic had worked.

"I'm so damned fed up," he said, as Bentley began working on accounts again. "With the town and with myself."

"Yeah?" Bentley said. "You ought to hear the women who cook for me. To hear them tell it, they never had it so good. Their husbands are working and so are they. One of them has a boy who's a lifeguard on the new private beach."

"How about you, Bentley? Are you happy with things as they are?"

Wallace Bentley said softly, "I never made this kind of money before in my whole life. I've had to hire more help. I don't like everything about the set-up. I wish I didn't have to be a bouncer. Some girls quit working for me, because the customers we get these days may rough them up a bit. But I can always hire more girls."

"Until the town runs out of decent girls. Until they all move away with their families."

Bentley closed his account book. "Gerry," he said slowly, "quit whining. Why don't you face the cold hard facts? Maybe I've lost a dream or two—but believe me, I'm sleeping better, now that I've got some money in the bank. I'm making a profit, in spite of all I've laid out for improvements. I'll spread the costs over the next two summers—"

"You expect this to last through two more summers?" Gerry asked. "That's the catch, you poor sucker. How long will it last?"

"I'll worry when the time comes. Let me show you the new tank."

He led Gerry to the front entrance of his restaurant. The place was beginning to fill for dinner—Gerry's drunken sleep had lasted most of the day.

He noticed that the quietly dressed townspeople in suits and dresses were already outnumbered by the tourist crowd. The voices he heard were ugly and strident. At one point, he had to shove past two girls of middle age, wearing little more than too brief shorts with halters that scarcely confined their bulging breasts.

The tank at the front entrance was floor to ceiling, a kind of glass-walled closet with a solid door in back.

"Those glass walls are double," Bentley explained. "There's room between the panels for about a foot thickness of water. When the lining is filled, anyone in the tank will seem, from the outside, to be immersed. Good trick?"

"Swell," Gerry said without heart.

"My girl will just sit there, naked. The water will be cloudy, a milky color, so no one will see her plainly. But it won't be fake, she'll really be naked. The only trouble is, I haven't got a girl yet to take the job."

"I'm not surprised."

"Someone will do it," Bentley said, "for a price. You'll see." He paused. "Gerry," he said suddenly, "have you seen a doctor lately?"

"No. Should I?"

"I think you should," Bentley said. "I think you're a sick boy."

"It's a thought," Gerry agreed vaguely. He left the place where once he had danced at his wedding. There was nothing left for him here.

For no special reason, he drove slowly home.

That night he had dinner with his wife.

Alice echoed what Bentley had said. "Gerry, you ought to see a doctor. You've acted so oddly the last few weeks. I've been frightened. I almost expect you to wander off, forgetting your name and address."

"Sorry, not yet," Gerry said. "I'm sticking around to see how fast Merton goes to rot."

"In that case, you'll be here for years." Alice's eyes flashed stormily. He had angered her, he realized. "This town is beginning to look like the old Merton again, with people coming and going, bringing in something new. This is the way life ought to be. This is the twentieth century, not the eighteenth."

Gerry laughed aloud. "You ought to look at the beach at three in the morning—you'd find lots of life, all right. But I doubt it's the kind that's changed in the past thousand years."

Later, he spoke alone with Grace Troy. "People are leaving town," she told him. "I heard today that Tom Simms will move. His wife is my cousin."

"That's too bad."

"Yes," Grace agreed. "Jane told me they felt it was best for their children to get away. Little Doug had been helping his dad take tickets at the dance pavilion and—well, he saw a lot too much, Jane said."

"They should have kept the children away," Alice said curtly, coming upon the conversation. "Children shouldn't be out at night anyway."

Grace waited. Then she said gently, "This was on Saturday afternoon."

"Oh." Alice shrugged, lost interest.

Grace continued, as placidly as though discussing the weather. "There are several houses on Third Street where towns-people moved out that went for a good price. They say the new owners are lesbians—that there's getting to be a colony of them in Merton."

Alice exclaimed, "That's a horrible thing to say."

"Why?" Gerry asked. "Because it's true?"

"Don't be an idiot," Alice said sharply. "Jack Chapin won't let the really undesirable element get a foothold. He knows his way around."

Grace raised her eyebrows slightly. Gerry reflected that Alice was probably right, certainly about Jack's knowing his way around. Gerry had counted on the law moving in. But what if

Chapin could buy the law, corrupt it as other persons and things were being corrupted?

Gerry spent the next two days at home. Grace cooked good meals for him. He spent time in the back garden, accomplishing nothing but rest. He thought of Louise but did not feel like seeing her immediately. She knew he was married, yet she had let him make love to her. He was a little afraid of Louise Edwards. On the third day after his homecoming, he went to see Jean Moore.

He had grown hungry for Jean, for her big full breasts, her forgiving comforting presence.

In front of Jean's house, he had an unexpected shock. House painters were swarming over the shabby frame building, turning it from grime-white into deep strawberry pink. The color, he thought, was crazy.

When he finally decided to go inside and ask Jean what was up, he had to use the back door. The front way was blocked by a scaffold stretched across two ladders. In the kitchen he stared incredulously around. Jean's new color scheme was something out of a nightmare. He peered into the living room where painters worked at the walls. Red walls?

Jean came from her bedroom and saw her caller.

"Why, Gerry." She smiled her unchanging, uncritical smile. She was wearing a sharp new outfit of tight orange toreador pants and a red-and-orange blouse. Her hair, newly dyed titian, was tightly curled. She looked as bizarre as her house.

"What are you up to?" he asked.

One of the painters hooted. His partner shushed him. Jean said like a happy child with a new toy, "Let's have some coffee." She closed the door between living room and kitchen. "Sit down, honey. I'll have coffee in a minute."

He sat. "Jean," he demanded, "what is going on? Where did you get the money to decorate your place?"

"I'll tell you all about it, honey. Just be patient." A little smile of happiness lifted the corners of her mouth.

He waited, with a semblance of patience, while she made coffee and slowly poured it. He accepted the cup. "Now, sit down and tell me what's going on."

"Just another minute, Gerry. Drink your coffee. The painters are about ready to quit for the day."

She tottered to the door and he realized she was wearing stilt-heeled orange shoes, not the flats she usually preferred, and which would have been right for the pants. She spoke to the painters, authority in her voice.

"Two more days? See that you're done. I want to get my drapes up before the weekend. Okay, good night. See you boys tomorrow."

The painters left, laughing among themselves. Gerry had recognized none of them. Were they from out of town? Where had Jean found them?

Jean sat down. She kicked off her shoes automatically and flexed her feet with a sigh. "Gee, it's tough to make a good appearance," she said brightly. "But it'll be worth it."

"A good appearance?" he marveled. He thought she looked grotesque but did not say so.

She laughed and patted his hand, her blue eyes excited. "Isn't it thrilling? All the changes in little old Merton. I never dreamed so many changes could be made in such a short time."

She was nervous, excited, wary of Gerry. He sensed her inner turmoil as she chattered on and on about changes in Merton, not mentioning the most flagrant change, which was occurring right here. He sipped his coffee, listened, trying to get a clue in her bright blue eyes, her nervous speech.

"Are you taking boarders?" he asked again, as she showed no signs of getting back to the subject.

"Well—yes, you might say so. I'm fixing up the bedrooms upstairs so you won't know them. Come on, Gerry. See all the changes I'm making."

He went up a narrow stairway with her to the second floor. Her bedroom had been a large room in the front with a view of the town. The room had been painted gold, with red trim. The floor was also gold.

"This is the gold room," Jean said proudly. "I'll have thin red drapes over the windows, a gold lamp beside the bed. All new beds, Gerry. I've ordered them from the city."

"No kidding," he said. A strong suspicion was growing in his mind.

They went to the next bedroom. This one was blue and gold, not quite so gaudy as the first, but still far from normal. Jean prattled about blue drapes, a gold lamp, a wide bed. She took him to the third bedroom, which was purple and gold. Worse than the other two, he thought, but Jean was even more proud of it.

"Won't they be pretty?" She sighed happily, and clasped her hands over her plump waist, which was belted uneasily into the tight toreador pants. "I'll have the bedroom in the back. But it won't be so fancy. Just a nice place for me to rest."

"For you to rest," he echoed.

"Then I'm turning two of the rooms downstairs into bedrooms. The back parlor and the sewing room. You know. One will be green and gold, and one will be red and gold like the front bedroom. Five rooms," she said.

"And who will be in those bedrooms?"

"Why—ah—boarders." She did not face him.

"Boarders. Women?"

"Yes, of course, women."

"And they might have gentlemen guests?"

"Why, sure, Gerry. All ladies like to have gentlemen guests."

"Especially in a whorehouse?"

"Oh, Gerry." She pouted. "Don't call it that. Mr. Chapin said it would be a very nice house, and I could run it very decently. He has faith in me."

"Jack Chapin planned this? He put you up to this? He encouraged you to run an out-and-out whorehouse?"

"Gerry honey, I have to earn a living. Merton is getting darned expensive. You wouldn't believe the cost of groceries now. I went to get some eggs yesterday. I declare, they cost ninety cents a dozen."

"Jean, how could you be such a damn fool?" He was saddened rather than outraged. "You're going to be a madam—you, of all people. Chapin flatters you and tells you lies."

"Gerry, he loaned me the money. He's a businessman. He wouldn't put out money like that if he didn't expect me to make good. I'll make lots more money than I ever made in my life. I won't have to turn a hand, so to speak—all I'll do is employ five girls, sit back and watch the dollars roll in."

"I see," he said. Maybe he was the crazy one and people were right to tell him to see a doctor. Everyone made it sound so logical to make money on tourists. Consider the price of eggs—the cost of running a business. Maybe he ought to go down to the lake, stake out his claim and go into business like all the others.

"I can pay Chapin off in four months, I figured out," Jean confided her plans. "Men don't mind paying high prices for really good girls. And Chapin will help find the best."

Briefly, Gerry closed his eyes, to shut out the gaudy and insane world.

"Don't be mad," Jean coaxed, leaning against him enticingly. "It won't change things for us. You can come in the back way, right up to my bedroom. I'll always take care of you, just like the old days. We won't change, not you and me, honey."

"We've already changed," he said. "Goodbye, Jean. Good luck."

"Don't go," she pleaded. "You've only just gotten here. We haven't had any fun—"

"Goodbye," he repeated. He kissed her forehead and left.

What was the point in his seeing a doctor? Any doctor in Merton would be like all the others, convinced that the town was booming, that prosperity was here to stay forever.

Any doctor in town would certify that Gerry was out of his mind.

CHAPTER TWELVE

THE more Gerry thought about Jean Moore and what Chapin had done to her, the more frightened and angry he became. In Jean's grotesque destiny, he thought he saw the reflection of his own. In a town that slipped downhill with gentle melancholy, there had been a place for Jean, a place for Gerry. If Jean had been the town whore, she had at least held the position with privacy and a kind of innocence. As for himself, he was a well-born unemployed dreamer. In the garish light of progress, Gerry also was grotesque.

Without consciously thinking of where he was going, Gerry headed for the lodge, driving on the lake road. It was evening, and tourists were lounging in front of their cabins. They were, characteristically, briefly dressed. He disliked looking at them. Most of them were not things of beauty. One man in short shorts pulled over a sagging belly with his upper body and legs a brilliant lobster-red from too much sunshine, seemed to embody what was wrong with the whole project. The women stared at Gerry with frank curiosity. He wondered if they knew who he was and that he had no job—that his wife no longer respected or needed him.

One long black car out of Chapin's automotive fleet was in the driveway at the lodge. Gerry parked his shabby sedan and charged into the main room of the lodge.

The only sound was the clicking of a typewriter, coming from another room. He found Louise Edwards in a small screened study. She glanced up from the typewriter and gave him a warm smile.

"Why, Gerry, how nice to see you," she said, with obvious pleasure.

Jack Chapin sat beyond her near the window. His bulk made his small desk seem even smaller. He swung around, said, "Well, Gerry Franklin. Haven't seen you for quite a while."

"I've been watching your work," Gerry said thoughtfully. He picked up a straight-backed chair, turned it backwards, straddled it as he sat. "I've been watching this town change. Congratulations on a very thorough job."

Chapin's face showed no emotion. "Have you come to needle me?" he asked.

Louise was staring worriedly.

"As a matter of fact, I was wondering whether to beat you up," Gerry said. "That's a laugh, isn't it? Because what would be my reason? Hell, why aren't you laughing?"

"Because," Chapin said, "you're a lousy comedian. If you think beating me up will change Alice's feelings, go ahead and try it. You might get smeared but that's the chance you take."

"I'm not discussing Alice," Gerry said. "I'm talking about Jean Moore."

Chapin's poker face finally showed amazement. "Scarlet sister Jean—you mean, you care more about the town bawd than you do about your wife?"

"I mean I care about the town. Alice knows what she's doing. But Jean doesn't. She's a country girl, no matter what else she is. She's gullible. She's swallowed your promises—she's turned her house and herself into lurid caricatures. And your promises are damn lies."

Louise gasped. "Gerry, please."

He ignored her. "Maybe I'm a fool," he told Chapin. "I'm fighting for the right to go to hell in my own way, not yours."

"I'm tired," said Chapin, "of listening to you. Okay, you don't like me. But I'm bringing business to your miserable town. What's your beef? Do you want me to go away, let the town die quietly? Is that what you want?"

"You're smart enough to know what you're doing to Merton," Gerry said fiercely. "Drive along the lake. Think what it was before you came. Look at the fishing pools and the big admission charges for things that were free before you came. Swimming pools, with women lying together on the sand where kids can gawk at them. I know lesbians when I see them, and I don't like their looks."

Chapin shrugged. "You've always got that element in a resort. The important thing is keep it under wraps, under control. I'll speak to Ted."

"Who are you going to speak to about Jean Moore? All she ever owned was her house—the house she was born in, by the way. You've loaned her lots of money, put her in debt to you, just so her house would be somewhere to place your girls. She shouldn't owe you a nickel—you should have paid her to do what she's doing to herself. Where do you think you're pushing her? You know this town won't last long. She'll get sky-high in debt, get herself a reputation from one end of this state to the other. After everybody pulls out, she'll have the rest of her life to live alone. You're ruining her life. Maybe you thought it was ruined to begin with, but you were wrong. She's a nice woman. Strange as it may seem to you, she has had friends."

Chapin seemed actually moved. "I didn't know she was a friend of yours," he said. "Ted pointed her out to me—"

"And Alice pointed her out to Ted," Louise added quickly.

So Alice had put the finger on Jean. At last he seemed to be probing, Gerry thought unhappily, the mystery of Alice. He said, "I want you to go to Jean and tell her the deal's off. I'll pay you back somehow for the money she's put into the house. But don't let her go any farther with this mad project."

Chapin laughed. "The decision was hers. If you want her out of the deal, talk to Jean, not to me. Persuade her yourself. I told her what the deal was. She accepted it."

"Children accept matches. A baby will play with a loaded gun. Come off it, Chapin. Don't play the innocent with me. You know what you're doing to people. Talking Wally Bentley into putting a nude woman at the entrance to his restaurant—talking the people into renting their cabins for immoral purposes. The lesbians have taken over one whole street with your help and connivance. The decent people are leaving town. By next year or the year after, Merton will be a ghost town, with a few derelicts left, the ones who ran out of money and got trapped. That's what you're making of my town."

"Now, look, Franklin—let me talk." Chapin pounded his desk and glared. "All right. So it's a rotten crowd of tourists. What choice do I have? This is what always happens. You build up a resort, provide fun and amusements, and riffraff moves in. It happens every time. Don't blame me. There are people who go where the fun is—and I didn't make them what they are. This is my job, building resorts. What am I supposed to do—get myself an organ and lecture from the dance pavilion about good boys and girls not getting into trouble? Hell, no. There's no choice."

"There was a choice," Gerry said. "There isn't a choice any longer but there was once a choice. We wanted to make this a decent inexpensive family resort, with free fishing, supervised swimming—" he broke off. "I'm tired of looking at the picture," he said. "Only a dream. Forget it."

The two men stared at each other. Chapin looked thoughtful. Finally he said, "I know the picture you mean. It might have worked. But it would have taken years."

"The people had years to spare. They wanted to stay here the rest of their lives."

"They all seemed willing to do what we suggested. They didn't protest."

"Their kids were hungry. They were out of work. They wanted to believe you, and you lie very well."

"They should have known the score. I thought they wanted to take quick profits, and then to clear out."

"Get out of their own town?"

Louise rose from her typewriter. She moved toward Gerry, tugged gently at his arm. "Why not come to my place for dinner?" she suggested. "I think you haven't been eating again."

He grinned at her. She looked so earnest and wholesome, with those freckles. "Sure I eat. Every once in a while."

She grinned in return. "Take me home, Gerry."

From his chair, Chapin watched them leave. "Good night," he said politely, as though from a distance.

"See you tomorrow," Louise replied.

In the car, Louise moved closer to Gerry and touched his hand lightly. "I don't know how you did it," she said, "but you reached him."

"I did?"

"People don't realize what a moody person he is," she said. "Suddenly, for some reason, he respects your opinion, Gerry."

Gerry laughed. "The hell he does. He has no respect for a— gigolo." He spat out the word. "All my fine talk about working. He knows what I am, living off my wife."

"Don't be an idiot," Louise reproved him. "Everyone in town respects you. Everywhere we go people say, 'What will Gerry Franklin think about it?' They listen to you, they know you for a thoughtful man."

Her words soothed his ego. He wanted to believe her. But he had been ashamed too long. "It could have been that way," he said. "But after I married Alice, things changed. Everyone says I married her for her money."

Louise shook her head. "Nobody says that." She hesitated. "Want to know what they really say? You won't be angry?"

"I won't be angry," he promised.

"They say it's a shame you married her—they think she's been driving you crazy, keeping you from amounting to what you could have been. She isn't liked, Gerry."

He was silent, staring at the road without seeing it. Did the town feel that about Alice? What was she really like? Would he ever know?

At Louise's cottage, they dined on the porch once more, watching the speedboats on the lake.

After dinner, they talked idly of far-off things, avoiding mention of Chapin or Alice or Jean Moore by tacit mutual consent. Louise had apparently traveled considerably at one point in her life. She spoke of Italy and Hong Kong while the night shadows covered the pines.

Later they went to her bedroom. She went to bed with Gerry as naturally as though they had slept together for years—except that her body was shy of his at first. He had to caress her and coax her until she relaxed and was at ease.

In the darkness, with the wind coming through open windows and the stars brilliantly shining, Gerry found peace. Lake waters rustled against the beach and boats slapped at their moorings. His hands rested on Louise's silken body. He murmured to her sleepily and heard her whispered replies.

He knew that what he was doing was wrong and yet he felt no guilt. What had become of his morals—had they decayed with the coming of Chapin, the promoter, or earlier, during the slow, long death of his marriage and his hopes?

CHAPTER THIRTEEN

JACK CHAPIN could not rid his mind of the sound of Gerry's voice. The guy, he thought, was a nut. But a sort of authentic nut—not a phony pretending to be sane. In some curious way, the younger man seemed to symbolize all the down-at-heels country villages which Jack had introduced to the resort business. He was not only a spokesman for Merton, but also for Oak Bend and Old Bourne and Bakers Bridge, all of which Jack had revitalized and abandoned. Gerry was all the abandoned, debauched people, all over the map, turned into one man and inquiring, "What have you done to us?"

He paced for a long time, trying to forget.

Gerry was not a figure of power or authority, but he did have a quality that Jack reluctantly indentified as humanity. If Gerry were on his side, he knew, little though Gerry amounted to, Jack would have more feeling of confidence on this project.

Had Alice really been helping him? Looking back with a certain prejudice, Jack failed to recall a single instance when Alice's ideas and influence had been a real contribution. People showed her a grudging wary respect. They feared the power of her money.

Surprisingly, Jack had found her greedy for more money. He had had to hold her back from going too far too fast.

Gerry's remark about lesbians made him resolve to have it out with Ann Short. He guessed shrewdly that the hard-drinking blonde was behind any perversion which had come into the picture. Not for the first time, he wondered if a man ever found associates whom he could really trust.

He wished Louise were still in the lodge. She was good to talk to. It was so damn quiet here alone that he could not trust his thoughts. He had to have people around him, laughter, talk, life, to be at his best mentally and physically. His current state of mind was disquieting. Usually when he felt this way, he knew it was time to move on. But he was far from financially ready to move out of Merton just yet.

He took one of his cars and drove to Alice's place. He would talk to her, make love, forget his restlessness for a while. She owed him something for getting him to come down to this place.

One of his own big cars was already parked in Alice's driveway when he arrived. Ann and Ted Short were here. He had thought they were out of the city, lining up operators for their new pool concession.

Grace Troy came to the door when he rang. Her face was placid as usual. He wondered if she disliked him as much as Gerry did.

"Is Mrs. Franklin in?" he asked.

"Yes, Mr. Chapin. She and Mr. and Mrs. Short are in the living room." She indicated the room with a nod of her head, then retreated.

A burst of laughter came from the living room. Jack was startled. Alice was seated facing the door, her head thrown back with a kind of screaming gaiety. Ted, sprawled on the couch, was smiling with lazy satisfaction. Ann sat on the floor near Alice's chair, her blond curly head resting against the couch, her mouth opened with laughter.

Chapin walked in. "What's the joke?" he asked.

All three jumped in surprise. The laughter erased itself on Alice's face. She rose gracefully, came toward him. "Come in. Have a drink."

She had been drinking heavily, he realized. Her breath reeked and she swayed with every step. She had to catch his arm to steady herself. Had they been drinking all afternoon? The air was warm and close with the musk of liquor.

He poured himself a scotch from the growing array of bottles on the buffet. Formerly, there had been a bottle of scotch here and one of brandy. Now there were seven bottles in various degrees of emptiness. They must be experimenting.

Jack sat down in an armchair and eyed the trio with no good will whatever. He had hoped to find Alice alone.

Ted's blond curls looked more incongruous than ever above his thin red face, blotched cheeks and bleary eyes. Ann looked like Ted's unholy twin, the middle-aged lines of her face show-ing through heavy make-up, under the bobbing curls. Even Alice was older tonight, not young and mysterious. Her dark eyes were cold with awareness as she watched Jack warily over the rim of her glass.

There was a long uneasy silence. Jack sipped his drink.

"How did you make out in getting someone to handle the pool?" he finally asked Ted.

Ted flipped a lazy hand. "No one is interested around here. I thought I'd wire south for one of my old buddies."

Jack suspected Ted had not even tried to find a new employee. His anger spilled over. "What have you two been doing the past week? I haven't seen you at work at all. How do you expect to get anything done if you're drinking day and night?"

"This is the first I've heard you object to drinking," Ann said with a smirk. "Cool down, Jack. We do our work. You won't have any complaints."

"I have a complaint already." Jack watched her face. He made a wild stab of an accusation, based ninety percent on instinct, ten percent on that chance word from Gerry. "I understand you're sexing around the beaches—with women. Since when have you turned lesbian?"

Alice uttered a shocked little cry. The other two did not register a flicker of alarm.

"Don't be ridiculous," said Ted. He raised his right hand, wrist limp, fingers dangling. "I swear my wife is a very hot female in my bed. She never refuses my embraces. So help me."

"That wasn't what I asked." Jack was almost sure his wild stab had hit home. "I asked when she turned lesbian. Have I been blind all these years?"

Ann watched him like a snake, unblinkingly. "What's it to you what I do? You don't draw any lines, do you? Take any woman you want, don't you?"

"I draw the line at perversion and you know it," Jack roared in a sudden gust of rage. He stood up, slammed his half-finished drink on a table. "Damn it. I try to keep the resorts clean, and you have to foul them up when my back's turned. Damn you anyway."

Ted swung his feet to the floor, slowly sat up. "Hey now. Cool off, Jack. She doesn't do it much. Just has to have a little change now and then. Can't have life getting boring, can we?"

"You know how I feel about perversion. You know I want things clean enough so the law won't nose around." But more than the threat of police action was infuriating Jack. It made him sick to think of these people working with him and being perverts. He prided himself on knowing people. This pair had fooled him. They made him sick at his stomach.

"Don't be two-faced, Jack," Ann drawled. "Why should you have all the women?" She laughed softly and drunkenly.

"Shut up, Ann." Ted took Jack's arm confidingly. "She doesn't know what she's saying. I'll be responsible for her. There won't be any more of this, I promise."

"You bet there won't." Jack shook off Ted's hand roughly. "You're both fired. Pack your stuff and get out. I won't have perverts around. This business is tough enough. I'm giving you an hour to make yourselves scarce."

Ann lost her flip attitude. She shrilled, "You can't fire us—we're partners. Our money is in this. Tell him, Ted."

"Figure what you put in the operation. Sign over everything to me. I'll pay you off," Jack said curtly. "Okay—stay overnight. We'll talk at the lodge tomorrow and settle everything. Then you hit the road."

He walked out.

For hours he drove around aimlessly, fighting his furious rage. He hated being tricked. He had not figured on Ann and Ted Short keeping a secret from him.

He could manage without them, once he got over his crippling anger.

By ten-thirty he had calmed down enough to remember Alice. She must have been horrified and disgusted. And Jack had walked out, leaving her with that pair. Poor kid—she'd be frightened and upset. He had to go back and talk to her, possibly stay with her all night. It was pleasant to think of bringing her some comfort.

When he returned, Alice's house was dark. He walked all around the house, peered up at her eyeless windows. Should he waken her, ask her to let him in?

He heard music drifting faintly uphill. The sound did not come from the house. Curious, he walked through the bushes along a narrow path that led down to the lake—from here, a healthy stroll. The music grew louder as he approached the shore.

He stopped abruptly just short of the beach. The moon glowed brightly on rippling dark waters on the stretch of cleared beach, on three separate couples writhing in the sand to the rhythm that came from a small portable radio.

Sick, stunned, he turned and ran away. If he stayed he would vomit—or beat them all with his fists until they were crushed and dead.

He drove until he ran out of gas. He found a filling station, woke up the attendant for more gas, and drove on. The movement of the speeding car on an empty highway numbed his senses, until he knew, gratefully, that he could endure what he had just learned.

Alice Franklin, so beautiful, so ladylike, was as vicious as anyone he had ever known. Behind the mysterious, dark eyes lay wickedness for its own sake. He could understand and forgive her greed.

But her corruption put her beyond his comprehension. All the times she had been in his arms, had she been longing for Ann? No wonder he had had trouble rousing her—

He drove back to Merton in daylight. During his long hours of flight, a plan had taken shape in his thoughts.

All his life he had been cursed with companions like Ted and Ann Short. His destiny, it seemed, was either to attract evil people or to bring out the worst in those he met.

In his work, he did not try deliberately to degrade a community. Given half a chance, people degraded themselves. All Jack had done was to carry around the corruption from one place to another.

He wondered if it could work the other way—if given half a chance, people could also improve themselves.

He doubted it very much. People seemed to be made of dirt. That was the point he had wanted to put across to that nut, Gerry Franklin, with his talk of a family resort. He had to prove Gerry was wrong. He knew the way to do it, too—give the idea a try and watch it flop. He had money enough to indulge himself on merely proving a point.

Presently he went into the lodge and faced the reckoning with Ted and Ann Short. He could hardly wait to kick them on their way.

CHAPTER FOURTEEN

GERRY was not sure why Jack Chapin wanted him at the lodge. The man had given no inkling on the phone as to what was on his mind.

Jack greeted him heartily. "Come on in, Franklin. Look at what I'm working out."

Louise and Gerry exchanged quick glances but had no time for spoken greetings before Jack launched into an exposition of the scrawled maps on his desk.

Gerry bent over the maps. He recognized a resemblance to Merton, the lake and the surrounding countryside.

Jack said, "You started me thinking, Gerry. I've dropped everything for this plan. See—this is Merton." Jack swept his hand over the map to indicate the town. "Here we'll enlarge Joe's place—have to take out two houses for that. Make an old-fashioned ice cream parlor out of it, with small tables and curved-back chairs. Red-and-white striped curtains—big menus, big sundaes and sodas, a place the kids will talk about."

Gerry stared. "These are plans for a family resort."

"That's right, Gerry. I want to prove you're wrong and I'm going to play fair, pull out all the stops." He went on explaining the plans.

"Down the street, the movie theater. It's to be completely rebuilt. Thought I'd tear out the block of businesses and put a children's theater on the end of the street, with another one next door for adults. Out of town limits, a summer theater, with performances, say, on weekends."

"This will take money," Gerry said.

Jack laughed. "I want to build something that lasts," he said, "except that it probably can't be done. Nevertheless I'll try. I won't keep pouring money into the thing. But a couple of years' losses won't hurt me. Now over here—" Jack whipped from one map to the other.

"Over here—Bentley's restaurant. All changed. Peaceful murals. No mermaids. Maybe scenes from local history. Good music. At the dance pavilion—a couple of nights of square dancing every week. Hire a caller. Have a couple of places with baby-sitters, a trained nurse in attendance—"

"Wait a minute—you're going too fast. Why build on a mammoth scale? Families can take care of themselves. All they need is a cottage apiece, and beach space—"

Jack shook his pencil at Gerry. "You've got to plan big. Nothing worthwhile comes from planning small."

"Does it have to be a world's fair? People with families want a place to relax, not to celebrate."

"Who's planning this? I've built resorts for years. You can't tell me a thing."

They were into one shouting argument after another. Gerry insisted that things should be kept simple while Jack argued that families would not come unless they had something different from what they had at home. Gerry said it would cost too much. Jack called him a nincompoop who had no understanding of business.

Gerry finally gave up. "Well, anyway, we agree on one thing," he said, wiping his brow. "We agree that Merton will be a family resort instead of a sex circus. Right?"

Jack began to laugh. "At least we'll give it a good try. I'll need your help. I've fired Ted and Ann."

"You fired them?"

"I bought them out. Same thing." Jack waved impatiently. "They left yesterday. Forget them." He seemed unwilling to discuss the matter.

With Louise's eager help, Gerry and Jack worked on plans for the rest of the afternoon. Gerry persuaded Jack to calm down on some of his plans, to shelve others until the second summer. "It's almost August. Let's start slow this summer. We'll have some cleaning out to do before we can build."

Jack nodded. "Speaking of cleaning out, I've got some calls to pay up the beach and in town." From the way Jack frowned, Gerry could figure the calls would not be pleasant ones. But Jack would have the undesirables cleaned out in a week.

He wondered about Jean. Could he help her? If she toned down the crazy colors in her new decor, she could run a boarding house. Jean was a good cook.

At one point Louise was briefly out of the room. Gerry spoke to Jack about Jean.

Jack looked embarrassed. "Tell her the loan is on an indefinite basis. She can pay me back in ten years if she wants."

"She isn't the kind to run a bagnio," Gerry said. "Whatever else she is."

Jack did not look at Gerry. "You and she can work that out."

What did Jack mean? Suddenly Gerry wondered how much the other man really knew about Jean? Women seemed to be easy conquests for Jack Chapin. Perhaps he was better off not knowing too many answers, Gerry decided.

That night Gerry ate dinner with Alice and Grace, but barely knew they were present. He was thinking. After all the bitter years of idleness, it was intoxicating to have a function—to work, to plan.

Could supervised fishing parties be sponsored? Would they need more docks for boats? Canoes—instructors would be needed. Another instructor for swimming.

He was worse than Jack, he admitted to himself. His dreams were getting bigger and bigger. He could not stop. Every plan in his brain had to be explored to the last detail.

Better calm down, he advised himself. He remembered Wallace Bentley. Bentley might be relieved to be rid of his rougher customers, but he had put out a lot of money to alter his place. He might resent ditching it all, starting over again. He would need help, financial and otherwise.

Alice frowned at him across the table. "Gerry? Is it too much, to ask you to be civil at the table?"

"Well, yes," he assured her. "Tonight, it's too much to ask."

The Merton theater was old, but it was fireproof. All they needed to do was to change the movie programs more often.

Some of the cabins had been rented for the summer. People would want their money back if they were asked to leave. He would have to speak to Jack—

"Gerry, do you or don't you want coffee? Why don't you answer?"

"You're being very patient," he told Alice. "You're wonderful. Coffee. You decide."

The next morning Alice cornered Gerry in the hallway as he was about to leave for the lodge. She was taut with anger.

"Gerry, I demand you tell me what's going on. Did you convince Jack Chapin that he ought to change the resort? What does he think he's doing?"

Gerry looked at her questioningly. He said simply, "What's your kick?"

"Ted and Ann called me from a motel. Jack has kicked them out of town. Ann says it's because of something you said to Jack." Her fists were actually clenched. "Why are you meddling? Who do you think you are? You never got anything right in your life."

"Including my choice of a wife?" He apologized at once. "I'm sorry. That was petty. Please let me go, Alice, without making a scene."

"He's really going ahead with it, then? He's going to turn Merton into a frumpy Mommy-and-Poppy place?"

"Yes, he really is. We're going to feature an ice-cream parlor. No more beach parties lasting all night. No wild carnivals."

"How dull," said Alice coldly. "Well, I wish you luck. Have fun, you two. Have lots of fun."

"Thanks," he said, his suspicions aroused. When Alice took things calmly, she gave an impression of secretly plotting something that would explode later on innocent heads. Should he keep an eye on her?

Perhaps he was wronging her, he thought, as he drove toward the lodge. Their marriage had become a mockery in which they both behaved unjustly.

He looked at the lake and sky. Both were still beautiful. If Merton boomed and the boom lasted, maybe he and Alice could get back on a healthier footing. For one thing, he would have work year after year.

Maybe some day Alice would be proud of him and respect him.

In some ways she was curiously like her father and grandfather. Money was more than a commodity to Alice, it was an art form. Money spoke to her, and she answered. If she became convinced there was money in a family resort, she would help them.

He thought with a sudden pang of the time when he had loved her—and realized that love was over. They still might have a marriage and a life together.

Not love.

It was bad not to love. He felt indescribably deprived, homesick for an anguish that always had seemed on the verge of turning to joy.

There had been no joy. After a while, the anguish had ended. But now at least he had work and work made him feel like a whole man.

Much had happened to him this summer. In his desire to make Alice respect him, he had won back his own self-respect. But Alice no longer mattered.

The next weeks were the happiest Gerry had known in years. The days of August sped past, full of work and excitement. He made plans with Jack Chapin by day and spent his nights with Louise.

Louise too was excited about the change in project. "For the first time, I feel involved in something worthwhile, something that will last," she told Gerry one night as he drove her back to her cottage.

"I'm glad," he said. "I feel the same way. Working on something I like makes me feel so good I should sing. And I can't sing."

She laughed, tucked her hand in his arm and rested her honey-blond head on his shoulder. "I'm happy," she murmured. "It's a new emotion."

Some of the cabins they passed were recently empty. The people who had rented them had quietly been deemed undesirable and requested to leave, their money refunded.

"I hope Jack can clear a small profit on this, eventually," Gerry said, his thoughts never far from the day's work. "He claims there can't be a profit but I don't agree."

"Jack never loses money on anything," Louise said confidently. "He won't make as much as he's used to, perhaps, but he won't lose. In fact—" She laughed aloud at a random recollection—"This amused me. He said last week after he finished the remodeling at Bentley's restaurant that he wouldn't mind coming here for a vacation himself."

Gerry grinned at her. "Good. And how about you, Miss Edwards? Could we persuade you to spend some vacation time at Merton?"

"Try me," she murmured.

"Look at the water over there." Gerry pulled up to the road-side and stopped the car. "We've cleared away the fences and the fishing is coming back." He shielded his eyes against the broad low rays of the setting sun. "Someone there looks familiar. Well, I'll be damned—I didn't know Tom had come back."

"Who's Tom?"

"One of the guys who used to live here. His wife is Grace Troy's cousin. He moved his family away this summer. But here he is again. The word must have gotten around fast." Gerry was tremendously pleased.

He drove on to the cottage. They went inside to her bedroom. She undressed swiftly. Sometimes she surprised him with her avid hunger for him. Usually modest, once in a while she seemed so impatient that she could not wait for modesty.

He also undressed, never taking his gaze from her silkily smooth, tanned body. Her freckled face was burnished now, her blue eyes a deeper color. Her breasts were creamy white mounds, the tips pink. Her thighs were white, then abruptly tan. Her long legs were flexed.

Naked, he lay beside her. She rolled into his arms, her arms going eagerly around him. Playfully he decided to tease her, make her wait. Satisfaction would be all the sweeter if it were deferred.

He kissed her soft, red mouth, played with her breasts. She moaned softly, holding his head against her breast. He continued to play. She moved impatiently.

He kissed the smooth arm and shoulder he held, the inner curve of her elbow. "Stop playing with me," she whispered. "I need you—Gerry, how I need you—" Her arms went around him, frenziedly, desperately. Her fingernails bit at his shoulders and back.

He could no longer hold back desire. He pulled her closer, closer—they could not be any closer and still he strove to be nearer to Louise. They were tight, hard-pressed, closer than breathing, their pulses storming and drumming together.

An unbelievable moment came, nothing he could have foreseen, when they were so much one that he had a sense of escaping the prison of self, of tremendous ultimate triumph.

Nothing like it had happened to him before. He knew it could not be love—he was not in love with Louise, was he—but love could not be better.

They got up presently, put on shirts and shorts, had dinner, and lay under the pines for a while, talking intermittently. Her hand reached for his and they lay with hands clasped together. The touch seemed right for now.

It grew dark.

He stared up at the moon and wondered how long this pleasant state would last. Joy never lasted long. Something would come to destroy it.

"I'm getting chilly," she said. "That wind is turning cold."

"Okay. We'll go in."

They ran back to her cabin. She was right—the wind was cool for August. Soon it would be September, then October and Louise would be gone. Jack would not be staying through the winter. Gerry would have work to prepare for next summer, but work was not enough—

He sighed deeply.

"What's wrong?" Louise asked.

"Nothing. Let's go to bed."

They went into her bedroom. For a little while in her arms, he could forget the coming of winter, live for tonight. This was still summer and he had a beautiful woman in his arms.

CHAPTER FIFTEEN

GERRY went home briefly the next day. He had to get some clothes. Grace had done his laundry.

"You're good to me," he told her. "Don't know what I'd do if you didn't help me."

"You're welcome," she said. She hesitated, then added, "Are you going to keep on living this way—half here, half somewhere else?"

He said truthfully, "I don't know. I suppose so. For the summer anyway."

"Alice had a party here last night."

"Oh? Glad I was gone. Who was here?"

"Ted and Ann Short, for two. They're staying here, you know. They have bedrooms upstairs."

He stared in disbelief. Her lips were tightly compressed. "No kidding. What is Alice up to?"

"I know very little. None of it is good."

He was worried. Alice was in bad company—and no matter how he felt about her, he was the only person responsible for her now.

"There were some others, from town. The faster ones. Quite a gay time. Alice sure likes parties. She was angry that you weren't here."

"You mean she missed her unpaid butler."

"Well, yes," said Grace bluntly. "She wanted you here to get liquor and serve drinks. She asked Ted Short to do it and he turned up his nose. Gave her a jolt. She never realized what all you did for her. She never appreciated you before."

Gerry was silent. It was too late for appreciation. He did not want to see or touch Alice right now.

But he saw her before he left.

"Grace says you had a party last night, and missed me," he said lightly.

Alice was chilly, unbending. "Yes. You don't burden yourself too much with your home any more, do you?"

"No. I've been pretty busy this summer." He paused. He hated parting from her on a sour note. "Jack and I are working out plans for next summer, you know. Takes time. There are a lot of details."

She looked at him strangely. "I'm surprised at you, Gerry. Do you really like to work?"

He was shocked. "Good lord, what have you thought of me all these years? Did you think my looking for jobs was an act? Quite an act—to humiliate myself over and over begging guys to give me a try. And then you'd come along and see that I got fired."

"You don't need to work for anyone else," she said crisply. "There's plenty for you to do for me. We could make a good team, you and I. I have money to invest that you don't even know about. We could work together. You have ideas too, Jack says."

It was as much as she had ever conceded to him.

"Thanks, Alice. I like to work. But I know I can work with Chapin. He respects me. I'm not sure you and I would ever agree."

"You mean that I don't respect you?"

"You never did."

Her dark eyes mocked him. "There never was much to respect, Gerry. Maybe things have changed. Why don't we give it a fresh try?"

Two months ago he would have been wild with joy at her words. Now he felt nothing but fear. He did not want to resume intimacy with her, he found. To touch Alice would seem disloyal to Louise. Crazy, he thought. His instinct was to be loyal to his mistress, not to his wife.

"I can't now, Alice," he temporized, to save her feelings. "I don't have much time for social life. I'm busy night and day, working on the resort. Why don't we wait till next winter, see how things turn out?"

Her eyes turned hostile. "Putting me off, Gerry? You've ignored me all summer. You've done things behind my back. Don't think I'm blind. It's bad enough to explain to guests that my husband doesn't know I'm giving a party. It's bad enough to be host and hostess both. But now you tell me you'll talk about it next winter? Well, I'm fed up right now."

Gerry cut her off hastily. "I don't want to quarrel. Do what you please. Throw my clothes out of the window, if it makes you feel any better. But I have work to do."

He left abruptly. He hated quarreling with her. She would get over her bad temper but only until the next time. No matter what role she offered him in her life, she would make him feel like a butler.

They could go their separate ways from now on, as far he was concerned. She would get used to his being away. Would they eventually get a divorce? He had not given the matter thought but he soon might have to.

He did not see his wife again for a week.

One afternoon at the lodge, Louise gave him a message that Wallace Bentley wanted to see him.

"He's been calling every few minutes. He sounds frantic. He wanted you to come right over as soon as you get the message."

The message was uncharacteristic. Gerry and Jack had planned to go into town and look in at the theater. But Bentley never would have sent that kind of message if he had not been in serious trouble.

He told Louise in parting, "When Jack gets back, tell him I'll meet him in town."

"There's a party at your house," Louise said tactfully. "I believe Jack is going there at five o'clock."

Gerry went off scowling. So Alice was still throwing parties—and still seeing Jack. He wondered if they were still going to bed together—but he had abandoned the privilege of indignation.

At Bentley's restaurant, he went in the kitchen entrance as usual.

"Wally's in his office," one of the cooks informed him. She sounded discouraged.

Bentley sat behind his desk, looking years older. He said, "Hi, Gerry. Have a chair."

Gerry seated himself. "You look like you've been hit by a rock," he said.

"Yeah. Your wife threw it."

Gerry stiffened. "How's that?"

Bentley's face was white under the tan.

"I had to borrow to open this place for the summer, before business got better later on. I thought I could borrow from a bank. I couldn't—but they suggested Mrs. Franklin."

"I didn't know Alice had loaned you money."

"She's loaned lots of people money. She's got her fingers in lots of pies, Gerry."

"And you're in trouble."

"Right. I'll go on with the story. When Teresa Brent told me how to redecorate, I said to Mrs. Franklin that I'd need more money. She loaned me more. I owe her nine thousand now. She has a lien on my restaurant for that amount."

"Wow," Gerry said simply.

"A couple of weeks ago I started paying her back. Made me feel damn good. I paid back a thousand in three weeks. I figured I'd be out of debt in a couple of summers and on my feet again for the first time in years."

"Yeah."

"This morning, Alice told me she was taking over the restaurant. I said, 'You're crazy, give me time to pay you back.' Ted Short was with her. He laughed. He said, 'Time, who's got time?'"

All Gerry could think to say was, "But Alice can't run a restaurant—"

"I called you. You weren't there. I called some other guys. All day I'm hearing the same thing. Alice Franklin wants to take over their places. She and Ted Short are buying up—or foreclosing on—houses, lots, beach fronts. She bought out nine people today. She wants to get her hands on everything here—fast."

All this had happened before, Gerry heard himself think. This was how defeat must have tasted, nearly seventy years ago, to another Franklin fighting another Merton—old Ben—for the soul of a town. A town called, in those days, Green Hope.

"What are you going to do?" he asked Bentley. "What are the others going to do?"

Bentley shrugged helplessly. "What can we do? We're over a legal barrel. You know the bank doesn't want to do it, but if she demands her money, they will have to foreclose. We signed notes."

"I'll stop her," Gerry said. He had no idea how he would make good on the promise, short of mayhem.

"Thanks, Gerry," Bentley said. Gerry knew the man did not dare ask questions—what Bentley wanted was a hope he could hang onto.

"You've got to help me," Gerry said. "Make me a list. Write down the names of the places she bought today." He strode restlessly as Bentley worked with paper and pen.

Bentley handed over the list. "Good luck," he said.

"Thanks. Tell your friends to sit tight. No rushing in the morning to sign any papers."

"I'll get the word around." Bentley looked more hopeful. The confident set had returned to his shoulders.

On his way home Gerry wished that he too could be hopeful. Much depended on Chapin's reaction. In a showdown, whose side would the promoter be on—with whose interests would he identify?

He drove up in front of his home, parked behind Chapin's huge black car. There were several other cars—a medium-sized party was in progress.

He strode in. Grace Troy met him at the door. "Hi," he greeted her. "If you don't like explosions, better stay out of the way. Tonight I howl."

"Did Bentley reach you?"

"Yep." He pushed her gently aside and went into the living room.

There was a crowd. Jack Chapin glowered from his chair, his hand clenched around a glass. Louise sat nearby, her freckled face taut and troubled. Ted and Ann Short were on couches at opposite ends of the room. They looked uneasy, Gerry thought. Teresa Brent sat in a straight chair, aloof and regal and slightly drunk. Bill and Patricia Rand lounged on the floor, propped on cushions. Alice was near Ted. She wore the silver lamé that Gerry had come to detest.

"Why, Gerry darling," Alice drawled. "You have condescended to visit your very own home. What a lovely surprise."

Ted Short laughed.

Gerry said, "Hi, Short. I thought you'd been kicked out of town. What brings you back, as though I need to guess?"

"Gerry, I won't have you rude to my guests," Alice launched herself at Gerry. "You're drunk. Get out and sober up."

"I'm not drunk," he said with deceptive mildness. "What do you mean by foreclosing on property owners, Alice?" He turned to her guests. "In case any of you think that my wife is working with you, wake up, friends. Alice works for herself. Today I found out what she's taking over, or trying to take over. Here's the list." He tossed Bentley's memo into Jack's lap.

Alice shrieked, reached for the paper, but Jack held her at arm's length. He stared at the paper, then uttered an awed oath.

"You fool," Alice moaned at Gerry. "You utter damn fool. We can make a fortune. Why can't you keep your mouth shut? I'll fix you for this."

Jack Chapin looked up from the list. "Alice," he said, "you're a bitch. I warned you. Double-cross me, and you're out in the cold."

She turned on him. "Out in the cold? Aren't you forgetting this is my town? I invited you here and I can kick you out."

Chapin walked over to Ted Short, bunched the back of the man's shirt in one fist. "I told you once before," Jack said, "to stay out of my sight. You and Ann—get. Now."

"You can't make him leave," Alice gasped. "This is my house—my guests."

But even as she spoke, Ted and Ann had walked out of the party. A car motor sounded outside, loud in the sudden silence.

"They weren't tough enough, anyway," Alice said aloud. She sounded not quite sane. "The hell with you all," she told her remaining guests. "This is my town and it's going to stay that way. Good night, and damn your eyes."

Imperious, erect and profoundly drunk, she stalked out of the room and went upstairs, a moving pillar of silver lamé.

"Dig that," said Bill Rand lazily from the floor. "Unfriendly little critter, isn't she?"

"We're in for a fight," Chapin said happily. "It was getting pretty quiet around here." He beamed at Louise. "I feel better. Hate to be bored." He slapped Gerry's shoulder. "Here, have some of your own good liquor. We've got a war on our hands. And I hate to face a war cold-sober." He raised his glass. "To a good battle, friends."

Bill, Patricia and Teresa drank the toast. Louise looked at Gerry meaningly. He went to sit beside her. The last thing he needed now was a drink.

CHAPTER SIXTEEN

ALICE was too quiet and amiable for the next few days, as though the stormy scene at her party had never occurred. Gerry hung around the house waiting uneasily for some belated violent reaction. He told Jack that he meant to keep an eye on her.

"All right, if you feel it's necessary," Jack said with a shrug. "I think you overestimate her ability to operate."

"And I think you underestimate her ability to hate," Gerry said.

Five days later a new man appeared. Chuck Trenn.

Gerry asked whether Jack knew him.

Jack did. "The little hellion got herself another fighter." He was evidently impressed. Trenn and he had fought before, he admitted. "He's a tough quiet dynamic man, thinks only about money. He can be deadly. But he's also practical. Soon he's sure to see he'll be losing this fight. He'll pull out."

Gerry was not so sure. He went home to dinner. Chuck Trenn was there, smoking one cigar after another, his black eyes sharp on Gerry and Alice. He refused to talk business while Gerry was present.

"We'll chat later when we can be private," he said to Alice, right in front of Gerry. "Your husband is working with Chapin, isn't he? I don't aim to tell Jack Chapin all my secrets."

"Gerry will be on our side presently," Alice said. Her eyes mocked him.

"I doubt it," Gerry said.

But he did not feel confident. For one thing, Chapin got bored easily. He had said so himself. Would he get tired of pouring money into Merton if another place called?

What would happen if Chapin left? Alice owned a large piece of the town and lake front. She would run the town as her father and grandfather had done. And Gerry would have to leave. He could not stay and remain under her thumb if she won out this time.

The next day, he found Chapin full of new plans. "We've got to do something big, something that will crowd out Trenn," Jack said. "Let's order a map of the town and the lake and indicate who owns what, as up-to-date as possible. That damn Ted Short didn't give me all his deeds. He kept some or sold them to Alice."

"I'll handle it," Gerry promised. He wondered how available all the facts would be—and said so. "There's such a thing, you know," he pointed out worriedly, "as dummy ownership. I'll look into anything that seems to smell of it."

"Fine," said Chapin absently.

For several days, Gerry looked into land titles. He made two trips to the county center to consult the records on file there, as well as asking a good many questions in town. On his first trip, Louise accompanied him. On the second, Chapin could not spare her time. Chapin had gotten involved with the bank in a three-cornered deal deriving from the remodeling of the movie house.

"Said the legal papers would take some time," Chapin explained. "I'll need Louise for typing reports and contracts."

Gerry found he missed her badly. She was so easy to be with that he had not been aware of the difference she could make. Like sunlight, she was readily taken for granted.

As he drove alone on the road where Louise had been with him earlier in the week, he was surprised at how clearly he recalled small things she had said.

I like you better now, she had said, *than I did when I first met you. Know something, Gerry? It's hard to like people who don't especially like themselves. And it's hard to like yourself before somebody likes you first. So there's a kind of vicious circle until somebody—a saint or a fool—breaks through. I ought to know,* she had said. *I've been unlikable in my time.*

Next day, he found Jack in a good mood at the lodge, but serious.

"I'm not satisfied with what that chart shows, Gerry," he said. "Alice has her hands on half the land in town. How did she get so much so fast?"

"Her father's money," Gerry said. "Some of the money has been owed for years. The bank loans it out, Alice signs the notes. Some people didn't even realize until this week that Alice was really the one to whom they owed money. They thought they owed the bank."

Jack shook his head. "Well—let's keep working. We don't have much time. The bankers can't stall off Trenn. He wants to buy out nine pieces of land along the beach."

Time was running short, Gerry thought as he drove home that night. He would rather have gone with Louise to her cottage, as she had suggested. But he had to keep checking on Alice and Trenn.

He had dinner with Alice and Grace Troy. They were all silent during most of the meal, apparently each in thought. After dinner, Grace disappeared and Alice said to Gerry, "Let's go in the living room, Gerry. We haven't talked for a long time."

"Okay," he said wondering what she was plotting. She sounded amiable and looked too beautiful.

She was wearing a soft green dress, the scoop neck showing her graceful white throat and sloping shoulders. As she seated herself on the couch, the sheath rode over her smooth knees. She made no attempt to pull down the hem. She patted the couch.

"Sit down with me, Gerry. Let's have a good talk."

He sat beside her. "What do you want to talk about, Alice? Money?"

"Don't be cynical, Gerry. We've fought enough about money. That wasn't the reason you married me, that's obvious." She smiled and put her hand on his arm. "I've teased you about it, but I knew all the time you didn't marry me for my money. But it was an easy weapon to use—and I managed to hurt you. I keep wanting to hurt you. I don't know why."

If she had talked so frankly a year ago, even three months ago, she could have saved their marriage.

"Why did you marry me, Gerry?" she asked, cuddling closer to him. "Tell me. What was the real reason? You obviously never trusted me. You refuse to spend the allowance I give you. You won't even drive one of my cars. Why?"

"I married you because I loved you," he said flatly. "Why did you doubt it?"

"Why not? Lots of people have wanted something from me— but why should anyone ever have loved me?"

"Don't tell me," he jeered, "that you're a poor little rich girl." He paused. "I guess you are, at that. I'm sorry, Alice. What do you want tonight?"

"You," she said. Her hand lay on his knee. Her eyes were filled with yearning. Was this his frigid Alice? "Gerry darling, we've missed so much—I've made so many mistakes. Please come back to me. Forget Chapin and his people—let's work things out alone, just you and I, Gerry."

"You and I and Chuck Trenn?" he asked, smiling in spite of himself.

"You're mean," she pouted. "Know something, Gerry? I think you still love me."

He watched her curiously. She stroked his knee with a kind of imperiousness. Her skirt was riding up, showing her lovely thighs. Her shoulder was against his, her breast pressed against his side. He had tried for so long to rouse this woman to passion. Now she was trying to rouse some passion in Gerry. An ugly thought crossed his mind. She would use sex as coldly as she had avoided it, to get what she wanted.

"Alice," he said, "it's hopeless. Don't make a farce out of what might have been a marriage."

"I've changed," she murmured.

"Who changed you, Alice? Where did you learn how vulnerable a man can be? From Chapin? From Ted Short? Or possibly even Ann Short? Let me say it straight. You make me sick. Your passion is fake. You don't care about anybody in the world but Alice Merton."

She flung away from him, dark eyes blazing. "You miserable excuse for a man," she spat at him. "All through our marriage I let you do whatever you wanted with me. And I hated it. I hate men. Wanting a woman, using her, flinging her aside—the way you threw me over for a woman like Jean Moore. And then that Louise Edwards with her freckles—But Chapin was even worse than you—making love, he called it. You know why I put up with it? I wanted him under my feet. Love? It's a beastly gymnastic, that's all."

He stood away from her. Suddenly he knew with complete certainty that she had been seeing a lot of Ann Short.

"You're a sick girl," he said. "You've got yourself a lady friend, haven't you?"

Her face twisted. "She's gone. You drove her away. You and that damn Chapin."

"I'm going too," Gerry said wearily. "I've had enough. Too much. Let's call it quits, Alice."

"That's fine with me—go ahead, move out. Get out of my house, I'm sick of you. I'm sick of all you men." She screamed the words after him as he left the room.

He ran upstairs to his bedroom, slammed the door to shut out the sound of her screaming.

After tonight, he would not return. He busied himself with packing, removing all traces of himself from this house, while the screams downstairs were followed by loud weeping.

Grace Troy came to his room. "Can't you help her, Gerry?" she asked, her kind face worried.

"I can only make her worse," he said grimly. "I think she'll quiet down after I leave. If she doesn't, call a doctor."

Suddenly the sobbing ceased. They heard a door slam. Grace said, "She's gone out. It's my guess she's gone to see the Shorts again."

"Are they still kicking around?" Gerry was not really surprised.

"They stay at a motel, not too far from Merton. She goes over there with Trenn."

"Oh," Gerry said. Grace might as well have been talking about a stranger instead of about his wife.

He cleaned out his room of clothes and personal possessions.

Grace helped him carry things in several trips to his car. Outside he said, "I'm sorry to be leaving you with the whole responsibility for Alice. She'll be rough to take care of."

Grace shook her head. "No, she won't. At least, not for me—I've always meant to leave some day and the day has come. I stayed, years and years, because of Alice's mother. I guess—I felt I owed that much. But I've done my share."

"Can you get another job?"

She smiled. "Wallace Bentley has been asking me to marry him since his business started looking up. Maybe I'll do it."

"For Pete's sake," he said. On impulse, he kissed her forehead. "Good luck," he said.

He drove away, knowing this departure was final.

CHAPTER SEVENTEEN

SUDDENLY the calendar said September. The world was still green but the nights were cooler, the days bright and brief. Gerry walked along the shore with Louise. They saw birds practicing formation flight over the lake, wild asters blooming softly in the brush.

Louise said in a practical tone, "The bank has been calling. They can't hold off Alice's claims much longer. Isn't there something we can do? The tourists have stopped coming. No one is making any money now."

"We can sit tight," he said with more confidence than he felt. "If we're losing ground, let's bear in mind that Alice and Chuck are also losing ground. Next summer could be worse for them than this one." The lake was too peaceful now. All the tourists had been dissatisfied in the end. Family groups had been frightened away by the rough crowd they had glimpsed. And the rough ones had been asked to leave, not in time to salvage Merton's reputation—merely early enough to leave the shore deserted for the balance of the season.

Bentley's business had gone way down again. He could not pay off more on his debt to Alice—in fact, he was going to need money to tide him over the winter. "What am I supposed to do, borrow more from your wife?" he had asked Gerry.

What they all needed was refinancing, Gerry thought worriedly. He wondered if Jack Chapin would be willing to stake Merton any further. It might be too much of a gamble even for Jack.

He asked Louise her opinion. She said, "I don't know, Gerry. I don't know what Jack's real plans are."

"It won't hurt to ask. I'd like to know at any rate if he means to stay another year. He never did say."

"It would be unlike him to pull out now. At least, that's what I think."

Gerry felt uneasy. He had better ask Jack outright, he decided, and get the situation out in the open. If Jack was unwilling to back them for the winter, they were finished.

Although the day's work should have been finished, Gerry went back to the lodge, to see the promoter. Louise said she would accompany him.

"Come in, my children," Jack said expansively, waving a glass. "I've been drinking alone and if there's one thing I hate it's drinking alone."

"Where are Bill and Patricia?" Louise asked. "I thought they were here."

"They were," Chapin said. "Now they're gone. I fired them. Teresa and I are the last of the outfit. She's in town."

Louise sank into a chair, her face showing a certain shock. "Will I be fired next?" she asked.

Gerry echoed her concern. "Does this mean you're pulling out? Quitting?"

"Quitting? Me? Hell, no. I'm just buckling down to a real fight," Jack said emphatically. "I found out today that Bill has been feeding information to Chuck Trenn and Alice Franklin. I can't afford disloyalty. So I kicked them out. Tired of them any-way. Fed up with Patricia. She's a stinker." He took a swallow from his glass.

Louise said cautiously, "Did you know that Ted and Ann are still around? They've been at Alice's occasionally."

"I know." Jack's voice was cold as metal. "Teresa told me, weeks ago. All of them, the Shorts and the Rands stabbing me in the back. At least you and Teresa stuck to the end."

"The end?" Gerry repeated the words anxiously. "End of what?"

"End of August, I guess. The fight has just begun. It's going to take more than will power to win. We've got to work with facts. The bank has to foreclose on Wallace Bentley. What can we do to stop Alice? Come on, let's get our brains together. I can't think alone."

Gerry blurted, "All right. I might as well tell you what I've been thinking. Those loans need refinancing. Will you put up the cash? Can you give people the money to pay Alice back and then forget for years that they owe you money? That's what it may mean."

Jack uttered a sound of outraged disbelief, then he said, "Come to think of it, that's a good idea. The loans are through the bank, aren't they? If the bank accepts the money, Alice will never be able to do a thing about it. The bank can't refuse to accept payment. Why didn't I think of this before? Baby, I'll fix you yet," he promised an imagined Alice.

Gerry's mood was sober. "We'd have to do it fast, all in one day if we can," he said. "We'd have to round up all her debtors and tell them what our plans were—but they'd have to keep a secret right up to the big day at the bank. If Alice gets wind of this, she'll foreclose so fast our heads will spin. The sheriff's an old friend of hers. We'll have to plan carefully and not let a word leak out."

"Can do," Jack said. He sat down at his desk. "I've got our list of people who owe her. Where's my pen? Why can't I ever find my pen?"

Louise handed him her own with a practiced gesture. Jack took a checkbook out of his top desk drawer and, consulting the list, began to write checks recklessly.

When he looked up, he said, "Have everyone come to the bank the day after tomorrow."

Early the next morning Louise and Gerry went to see Wallace Bentley, talked with him privately in his office. He readily accepted Chapin's check after they convinced him they were not perpetrating a hoax.

It took them all day to see everyone on the list. Oddly enough, they encountered more suspicion than jubilation. "People don't believe in Santa Claus any more," Louise complained, "unless they're either very young or very old and wise."

The following day, Gerry and Chapin were at the bank when it opened. Louise was with them, equipped with stenographer's notebook. They found three extra desks set up in the loan department. The president and vice-president of the bank were on hand to witness the multiple transaction.

Wallace Bentley came with the first arrivals. Notes were written up, signed, as old notes were written off. Alice's debtors entered, family after family, man after man, paying off old notes with Chapin's checks, then signing notes to be held by Chapin instead of by Alice Merton Franklin.

When the bank doors closed at three o'clock, there were still nine notes unclaimed.

The bankers decided not to lock their doors for another hour.

By four-thirty, the transfer was complete.

Chapin, suddenly poorer by eighty-five thousand dollars, said, "This calls for a celebration."

The party adjourned to Joe's Diner, now empty of customers.

But Joe had come to the bank in the morning and his place was securely his for the first time in years. He served soft drinks on the house.

"To the future of this town," said Chapin, raising his glass.

All of them drank to the town.

Later, Chapin said reflectively, as they went back to the lodge, "I'll have to find another place to stay. This is one piece of property I won't contest with Alice."

"Gerry, will you take me home?" Louise asked.

"Not yet," Chapin urged. "I want your help in bringing the map up to date."

Gerry had set up the map in the dining room, with property liens indicated by bright glass-headed pins—green for Alice, red for Chapin, white for free and clear. They made the changes corresponding to the day's business at the bank.

The difference was impressive. Chapin leaned over the table, grinning affectionately at Gerry's handiwork. "Look at that," he gloated. "Look at that—isn't that pretty?"

They left him to revel in red-glass pinheads. The austere Teresa had come to drink with him. He was not alone.

Gerry and Louise went to her cabin bedroom. A breeze from the lake fanned their warm bodies as they lay side by side. Both were tired. They did not stir at first. It was enough for them to be together.

"Autumn," Louise said dreamily. "I've always liked the autumn. It doesn't mock sad people—it goes along with them. What is winter like here, Gerry?"

"Ice on the lake, thick enough to skate on. Time seems to be slower. People make sure they have snow tires on their cars and plenty of oil in their tanks. You can see for miles, because the leaves are gone. The town gets quiet. When the snow is deep, everybody walks, wears boots and leggings. Sometimes the electricity goes off for a day or night. Then we use lanterns and candles."

She cuddled her head against his chest. "Sounds lovely. I wonder if I'll be here."

He wondered also. Would Chapin stay all winter—or would his restless mind and widely spread interests pull him somewhere else? Would Louise go with him? He had no right as yet to ask her to stay. He was still legally married.

To shut out unwelcome thoughts, he kissed and caressed her until they talked no longer. Hungrily, their bodies moved closer. They joined without words on the wide bed. Words would have destroyed them, made them sinners. Without words, here was rest and peace. Here was sanctuary. He never wanted to leave.

Louise was moaning softly under the urgency of his passion, trembling.

Then all was quiet once more and his breathing slowed and his pulse ceased drumming hectically. Now he could hear the lapping of the waters on the lake, the call of the night birds, the dry labor of crickets. He could hear Louise's voice, soft in his ears. He held her tightly, safe for another moment or two from the loneliness to come.

CHAPTER EIGHTEEN

A T the lodge next morning Gerry sharpened pencils and twanged rubber bands, waiting for Alice's inevitable reaction to yesterday's events. Louise was taking dictation in Jack's office. He heard the steady rumble of Jack's heavy voice, without making out the words.

He felt restless. There was little left for him to do until next summer. This was September. Nobody would come in late September to a new untried resort.

He drummed his fingers on the windows ledge as he looked out over the lake. What would he do all winter? What would Alice do? More important—would Louise stay? He wondered if Alice would give him a divorce and what he would do if she refused.

Was he crazy to dream? What right had he to expect that Louise would marry him? They had not spoken of marriage. She seemed thoroughly to enjoy working with Jack Chapin, traveling from place to place.

Jack had had a call from Florida a few days before. He had started sporadically talking about northern Florida and the possibilities there, almost at once. He would probably pick up and leave before long—and Louise would in all likelihood go along.

Then what? Back to Alice and a frozen truce? Or back to Jean Moore? He winced. Jean was sullenly angry at Gerry for wrecking her chances of making money. She had refused to make any changes in her house plans, had insisted that the painters continue as they had started.

But he was not in love with either woman. Emotionally, he was through with them. He stared unseeingly at the lake.

He could rent a cottage and get a job in town, maybe a job at the bank. More than a hint had been dropped yesterday that Gerry's employment application would be viewed with favor. A small town banker. Might not be a bad life. And if the town picked up, business would be good, the bank would grow right along with everything else.

Alice could not get him fired this time. She had a lot of money in the Merton bank, but so did Jack Chapin. That made a difference.

No one in Merton had to worry any more about antagonizing Alice.

A car door slammed outside. He ran to the front entrance in time to meet Alice coming up the steps.

She saw him and paused. They stared at each other, as though seeing each other for the first time. Alice was not looking at him as a potential suitor, as a fiance, as a husband for whom she felt only contempt.

She looked at him as an opponent who had bested her.

"Well, you pulled it off," she said. In spite of her obviously deliberate control, her voice shook with fury. "I just left the bank. Where's Jack?"

"Here," Jack said, appearing behind Gerry. He came forward, grinning. "I told you you'd know you'd been in a fight."

She glared. "So now you own more than half the town. You can wreck it any way you please."

"I've gotten bored," he said gently, "with wrecking towns. I'm planning to go to Florida this winter to start another family type resort. That's going to be my new line."

Chapin spoke with the untried fervor of a convert. In a quiet corner of his mind, Gerry wondered if families would ever be the same again, now that Jack Chapin, promoter, had turned his energies to building resorts for them. Perhaps the mother of the future would bring her loved ones to breakfast with a snappy fan-fare and a cry of *The show must go on,* rather than a simple *The eggs are getting cold* ...

"Come on in the dining room," Jack said to Alice. "Let me show you something."

She accompanied him, her face severe and frozen. Her hips swung definatly. For the first time, Gerry realized how much Alice had changed that summer. She had little trace of feminine fragility any more. Though she had lost this battle, she seemed to have retained confidence in herself.

The change was not becoming, he thought. It was ugly to see a woman out for blood. Was she going to prove that she could outdo her father and grandfather, that she was even tougher than they?

She looked at the map carefully for some time. "Hum. I don't own much any more, do I? You really cleaned me out. Well, do you want the rest?"

"What did you say?" Jack said. She had caught him totally unprepared for that sort of offer.

"No use in my staying here. I don't want to stay where I'm not the number one person," Alice said. "Want to buy my house and lodge and any other properties I still own in town?"

Jack gave her a hard look. "Keep talking," he suggested.

"All right." She sat down at the table, shoved the map a little aside and got out her pen. After making rapid figures on the edge of the map, she announced, "You can have the lot for two hundred thousand. That includes the house, the lodge, even the empty old Merton Mill—everything."

"You're crazy," Chapin told her.

She said belligerently. "You think it's too much?"

"No," Jack said. "I think it's a steal. Louise, bring my check-book. And Gerry—call the bank. Everybody's lawyer is on vaca-tion so we'll handle this little deal with a notary public."

Later, as the bankers were leaving, the bank president drew Gerry aside and repeated his suggestion. "Why don't you work for us, Gerry? You seem to be doing it anyway. You might as well draw a salary."

"I'll come in tomorrow and talk about it," Gerry said. They shook hands.

Alice said to Chapin in parting, "Now you own Merton. Hope you like it. Know what I'm going to do? I'm going in business with Ted and Ann and Bill and Patricia. We're going to build resorts like you used to, full of fun and fast times. We've got the know-how and the money. You can watch our smoke."

Gerry said with concern, "Smoke can cover a lot of trouble. You'll be in for plenty of it with that crowd." It was his last attempt to protect her.

"Let them look out for themselves," Alice retorted. "If I don't like what they do, I'll fire them. I'm going to be head of the company. Things will be run my way."

She might get burned, but others would be burned worse for dealing with her—and Gerry figured he had better accept the fact.

"Is Teresa going with you?" Jack asked.

Alice made a face. "No. She said she'd stick around with you for a while and see what happens."

"Good." Jack paused. Gerry, watching them, found it hard to believe that once they had been lovers. Jack held out his hand. "Well, good bye, Alice. It was a good fight."

She shook hands with him, turned and left.

"I'll see you to your car," Gerry told her. He wanted to talk to her privately. When they were outside, he told her, "You don't have to leave town, Alice. You could still go in with Jack. He's a good businessman and he thinks the world of your abilities— with direction."

"And be bored to death?" Alice laughed, slid into the driver's seat of her lemon convertible. "I'm running my own life now. I don't need your help. Anything I can do for you in turn?"

"As a matter of fact, there is," he said slowly.

"Name it. Some furniture?"

"No. A divorce."

Her anger flared. "So you can marry that Edwards girl? I might have guessed. You've been playing around with her all summer. That's what's changed you."

"Was it?" Gerry echoed mildly.

"Well, you can go to hell. I'm not giving you any divorce. You can go down on your knees and beg and it won't do you any good." She started the car. He stood back.

"I'll keep trying," he warned her. "Our marriage is over."

"You'll be crawling back to me, wherever I am," she predicted. "You won't find it easy to hold a job—I can still pull some strings, Gerry boy."

She drove away with a roar of the motor and a spinning of wheels in gravel. Jack Chapin came outdoors, clasped Gerry's shoulder lightly.

"She's a real hellion, Gerry. Don't worry about Alice, she's a lot tougher than you or I. She'll always come up swinging, no matter what she gets into."

"I'm not worried any more. But I want a divorce."

"Wait till she isn't so angry. She's taken a lot of body blows the past couple of days," Jack said. "When she cools down, she'll probably want a divorce herself, to marry someone else."

Gerry was not so sure. Alice might never want to marry again. A wedding ring still on her finger would be some protection from gossips. She had no real motive for giving him a divorce.

"Chuck Trenn, Alice's new promoter, called just now," Jack continued. "He wanted me to confirm what had happened. When I told him Alice had sold out, he said he was leaving town. I guess he knows what the score is."

Gerry stared out at the lake.

Chapin shook his head and returned indoors.

Gerry walked slowly toward the lake.

He felt numb inside. The crack-up of his marriage had come to a head this summer. At first he had loved Alice and later he had hated her. Now he felt sorry for her as she started out on her dangerous trail.

The town of Merton was safe, though, and he was grateful. He walked slowly along the shore, thinking of how it would be next summer. Families on vacation. Brown-skinned kids, the boys fishing, the girls swimming, the toddlers discovering wild flowers—

"Gerry?"

He turned at the call. Louise was at the driver's seat of his car, farther up the road. He climbed toward her up the bank.

"Jack gave me the rest of the day off, to celebrate. He's gone to find Teresa. Why don't we celebrate too?"

When he nodded, she slid over, letting him take the driver's seat. He started the motor.

"Gerry, what's wrong? Aren't you happy?" She tucked her hand in his arm.

"She won't give me a divorce." He stared straight ahead. He could not look at Louise.

"Oh." She put her cheek against his shoulder. "Maybe she will later."

"I want to marry you now."

"I think that's a lovely idea," she said, her voice a little ragged.

"But we can't—not until she lets us." He shook his head despairingly.

"Gerry, we'll wait. We have all the time in the world," she said comfortingly.

He did not want to wait. He felt he had already waited for years.

They went back to her cottage and made love through the long cool afternoon. It eased the pain inside him to hold her close and caress her.

But they could not belong to one another until Alice gave him a divorce. He longed for the one thing she had never wanted to cede to anyone at all—freedom.

CHAPTER NINETEEN

ALICE gave a party before she left town. Her guest list was an oddly mixed one—Gerry and Louise, Jack and Teresa, Ted and Ann Short, Bill and Patricia Rand, Wallace Bentley and Grace Troy were all invited.

Gerry wondered about attending. But Jack said, "Might as well go. Her liquor is always good."

For a while the party went well. The September night had turned warm. Couples wandered in and out of the house to the wide porch and the lawn, in search of some breeze to cool them. The liquor was good. Joe was there to serve it, Gerry was amused to note. Alice had had to find a new butler.

As a hostess, Alice resembled an amiable house cat, slinking around in a tawny cream sheath dress with green and gold jewelry. She seemed satisfied with herself—Gerry's skin prickled in warning. When Alice looked like that, someone was about to get hurt.

Jack Chapin danced with every woman present, including those he detested, apparently enjoying himself with his characteristic vigor.

Gerry danced with Louise, aware of Alice's narrowed gaze on them from time to time. He was afraid of talking to Alice, afraid of upsetting some delicate equilibrium in her emotions and bringing on trouble.

Ann was dancing a lot with Bill Rand and Patricia Rand was sulking. Patricia joined Gerry at one point and complained of Bill's behavior in a whining voice.

"He always goes after a woman when I don't like her. What makes men behave like that? All I have to say is I don't like a woman, and he goes after her."

"Too bad," Gerry said. Patricia was drunk and talkative. He listened with vague attention, watching Louise dance with Jack Chapin. He liked her freckled face and uptilted nose even when she was dancing with someone else. It was good, he thought, to be in the same room with her.

"Dance with me, Gerry," Patricia urged suddenly. She had her arms around him before he could protest politely that she was much too drunk to dance with.

He went once around the floor with her. Then she complained that she was hot.

"Let's go outside and cool off. I'm so warm. And I hate to see Bill with Ann. It makes me so damn mad."

It occurred to Gerry that the girl needed fresh air, quickly and in quantities. He took her outside.

She kept complaining until, bored, he said, "Let's go back in."

"Oh, I'm still hot." She took his hand. "Let's walk down to the lake."

Was she making a play for him? "I'm going back," he repeated. He turned toward the house.

"Gerry, you can't desert me now," she wailed. She flung herself at him. "I'm so unhappy."

His suspicions were aroused. She was play-acting. Why? What was she up to? He began to run to the doorway. Patricia tried to prevent him. He unwound her arm from his neck, pushed her crossly away. "Let me alone. I'm going back."

The couples were still dancing in the large living room. Jack was with Teresa, Wallace and Grace were absorbed in each other. But where was Ann? Where were Ted and Bill? Louise was nowhere in sight—and Alice was smirking.

He strode toward Alice, demanded, "Where's Louise?"

"Why the last I saw her, she went outside with Ted. The night is so hot." She was close to laughter. He would get nowhere with her.

He approached Joe, asked, "Have you seen Louise?" He heard a muffled cry from upstairs.

He ran, pushed open the door to one of the bedrooms.

Louise was on the bed, held down by force in spite of her struggles. The three he had missed from the group were tittering drunkenly. What they seemed to have in mind was Louise's submission to Ted.

Gerry picked Ted up and flung him against the wall. He shouldered Bill out of his way. Ann came at him like a cat, her heavily made-up face grotesque with fury.

Louise rolled off the bed, dashed for the door.

Jack Chapin appeared in the doorway. He roared, "What in hell's going on?" Ann turned on him and he slapped her face. He turned to Ted, who cowered back. "Don't hit me—don't—"

Jack used his thumb to indicate the door. He said, "Out."

The trio left. Gerry held Louise in his arms, soothed her hysterical sobs. There was rage in his heart. They had tried to ravish her, out of no motive but rottenness. The plan had been Alice's, he was sure.

"I'm all right," Louise said, minutes later, pushing her hair back. "It was such an ugly thing to happen. And they all laughed."

"Nothing happened," Gerry told her firmly. "You had a bad dream. Look, honey—let Jack take you home. I'll be along later. I have to talk to someone."

In spite of her protests, he insisted on her leaving with Jack Chapin.

He found Alice in the living room. He asked her a one-word question. "Why?"

"Why what?" she asked. She looked amused. She knew what he was talking about.

He said patiently, "Don't make me break your neck. Why did you turn those mangy dogs on my girl?"

She surprised him. She started to cry. "All I did was give a party," she said. "Suddenly I'm to blame for everything that ever went wrong since time began."

A man, he thought helplessly, could never really win a fight with a woman. All he could do was escape. He took a different approach. "I'm asking once more—will you divorce me? You have legal grounds enough, lord knows."

"You'd like that, wouldn't you?" she stormed. "Why should you be rewarded for being unfaithful to me? You deserve to be punished."

"I agree with you," he said, as though talking to an idiot or a child. "But you punished me in advance, Alice. I'll grant you couldn't help yourself. You made me feel I was less than a man—feel, hell—you turned me into a bum, eating off a woman. We're bad for each other, honey."

Her mouth tightened. She said nothing.

He tried cunning. "Maybe it's just as well for us to stay married. I've got ideas for using that small negotiable fortune you've just made in real estate. First, I'd like to start my own company, have a profitable little business on the side. Do you realize there isn't a single jeweler in this area who handles anything costlier than cultured pearls? I'd like to go in for diamonds."

He seemed to have reached her. "Diamonds? You? Around here? Are you out of your mind?"

"I'll double your money," he promised. "A jeweler could make millions here in the next ten years. We're going to have a carriage trade, once everyone is rich."

"You've got to be kidding," she said.

He shrugged.

"I think you mean it," she said excitedly. "This is one time you saw my money, instead of just hearing about it—when Jack gave me his check. You can't wait to ruin me, can you?"

"Now, honey," he said. "You know I'm a good businessman, given half a chance."

"You?" She looked terrified. "You can have that divorce," she said.

He thought wryly that she would believe anything at all which proved that people were after her money. In the final analysis, she was unable to believe in love.

Poor old Alice, he thought—poor old beautiful lost little girl.

In spite of the night's unseasonal heat, he tasted winter on his tongue.

Somehow the coming winter would be the most important one of his life—and possibly of Alice's life—and Louise's.

He reflected that it never was cheering to fail in a marriage, even a miserable one.

He folded away his failure in some private file in his brain and waited for life to resume. After a while he headed for Louise's cabin.

CHAPTER TWENTY

ONE night the full dark came by five-fifteen. Most of the bank personnel had left. The calendar on the wall said November.

Even after a month of working at the bank, Gerry was still surprised at the quantity of details which had to be tended to. Business in Merton had picked up a good deal. People were coming in for loans to expedite plans for next summer's tourists. But now it was evening and Gerry was alone in the bank.

Alone, he thought, in other ways too. Jack Chapin had gone to Florida for the winter. He might never be back.

Jean Moore had sold her house and left town, declaring plaintively that nothing was left for her here. He suspected that she had derived an emotional nourishment from being the other woman in his life—now that he and Alice had split up, she had felt restless in Merton. She had been good to him. The relationship was ended. But many things had ended this summer, with the coming of the resort.

Alice's divorce was not yet final—and, from the restlessness with which she changed residence, might never be final. In the end, Gerry might have to be the plaintiff, an ugly prospect.

He stood up, closed his desk and nodded to the guards as he walked out. One of them was a man he had gone to high school with.

The street outside was damp underfoot. Lights glowed with a halo. This was still a small town in November's dusk, where most shops closed at six. Next summer would be different—there would be life and light—traffic and heat.

The movie theater was open and Gerry eyed the posters with interest. This was one that Louise wanted to see. Maybe they could go tomorrow night.

Since Alice's departure, he had boarded with a local family. His quarters, newly decorated just this past summer for tourist rentals, were extremely comfortable and the rate, an out-of-season one, was moderate.

"Any message?" he asked his landlady.

"Yes, Gerry. A Mr. Lee just called, long-distance. You're to phone back at once."

"I'll call from my room." Gerry told himself to calm down. But the call was from Alice's lawyer.

He made the call, staring blankly at the wallpaper of his room. He was tired of living in a rented place, tired of waiting for Alice to take action. Tired of loneliness.

The call went through. On the far end, a man's voice said, "How's everything, Gerry?"

"You tell me," Gerry said.

"Good news, I think. Alice wrote from Florida that she got the divorce two weeks ago. She sent papers. I've gone over them. They're all right. But to make sure I called the court where the plea was granted. It's okay. You're all set."

Gerry sagged in his chair. He was so relieved, he was sweating. "Thanks for letting me know," he said. Two weeks ago. The delay seemed characteristic of Alice.

"I thought I should check thoroughly." The lawyer hesitated. "You can be quite sure she got the divorce—because she's married again."

"Married—Alice?"

"Yes. Some man named Blake."

"I don't know the name."

"Well, I thought you would want to know."

"I appreciate that," Gerry said. He wondered who Alice had married and then dismissed the wonder.

He showered and changed and drove out to the cottage. Louise was waiting for him with a good dinner.

"Have a good day?" she asked.

He had a sudden picture of their future, with Louise waiting at home for him, maybe with a baby later on. She would always say, "Did you have a good day?" and would listen sympathetically to the answer.

"I had a good day," he said. He took her in his arms, sensed her stiffen against him. He knew why—this waiting had told on her nerves.

He teased, "You'll have to start thinking of winter quarters. You can't stay here even as late as Thanksgiving."

"I know. I'll figure something," she said.

It would have been cruel to withhold the news any longer. He told her he was free.

She drew a deep breath, put her head down on his shoulder. She was trembling. "I was so afraid—so worried that something would go wrong."

"So was I, to tell the truth." He turned up her face to his. Her eyes were closed, and there were tears on her lashes.

He kissed away the tears. "Honey, honey."

"I'm so happy."

"We can get married. Maybe it sounds crazy—but I feel as though I hadn't been married before."

She laughed with joy. "I have to get a marrying dress."

"We'll go wherever you want and buy one."

"Come to dinner. This will be a feast, Gerry—a celebration."

They ate indoors. The porch had long since grown too cool for comfortable dining.

After the meal, Louise read aloud a letter which had arrived that day from Jack Chapin.

In the middle of it, Gerry interrupted, "Every new place is the place he likes best. He's a dynamo."

"He was a good man to work for. This is the part I wanted you to hear especially." She went on, "Tell Gerry I'm thinking of using his family's old name for the town. There ought to be a Green Hope Inn and a Green Hope golf course and maybe even a Green Hope Museum—tell him to think about it. When I come back in March, I want to see that name on signs."

Gerry felt enormously pleased. All he could say was, "I'll think about it."

They put on heavy jackets and went out to walk on the shore. The wind blew steadily, rippling the waters in chill black waves. Louise picked up a piece of driftwood. "I could whittle this into a paperweight," she said. "Our first wedding present."

"Good idea. From the lake to us, with best wishes."

She laughed and clung to his arm. "Why not? I've found what I want—right here."

He bent to kiss her mouth. "Me too."

They strolled a little longer, making plans without limit, until the chill drove them indoors.

Louise put her driftwood on a table. "I'll keep it the way it is," she said. "It's so nice and funny-looking—"

Suddenly she was in tears.

"What's wrong?" he asked in sudden panic, taking her in his arms. "Is it because I'm offering too little? Dearest, I'll work so hard. I'll give you the world—"

"No," she whispered. "Not the world. What I want is you. I'm crying because I'm happy—and life is so swift and sad."

"I know," he soothed her, not really knowing, not needing to know. Their bodies moved closer.

The wind was loud in the pine trees. Winter was near at hand. Soon ice would blanket the lake and the world would be white and hostile.

But he knew where the warmth would be. What else did a man need, except one woman's heart always warm for him? He had much to learn of happiness, he thought contentedly.

"Sweetheart," he told the girl in his arms, "suppose we go upstairs. Somehow I can't face being away from you tonight."

She sighed with pleasure and trust in him and let him lead the way.

THE END

www.ingramcontent.com/pod-product-compliance
Lightning Source LLC
Chambersburg PA
CBHW052011240626
47153CB00008B/2824